Song of Return

Laci Barry Post

For my wonderful, creative husband, Jason Post -
who made this book possible.

Chapter 1

September 28, 1946 - "They're here!" Grandpa Chester hollered from the swing on the front porch.

"Victoria!" Sheffield also called from outside.

Ava and Carson leapt up from their game of checkers and ran to the door.

"Not so fast." Victoria stopped her son and daughter. "Ava, stay here with Ella, and Carson, open the front door for us when we get back."

"But Mom, I can just carry Ella," Ava said picking up the unaware two year-old from where she was tottering on the floor with an old cooking pot.

"Let's not overwhelm the poor girl," Victoria ended the discussion. "You would have at least thought that he could have told us our new daughter-in-law's name!" she muttered, and the front door closed behind her.

Ava and Carson didn't leave the house, but they were certainly not going to miss the occasion. The letter had arrived yesterday. James was returning with a new wife! Ava placed her niece back on the floor and joined Carson at the oval window in the family room.

"Scoot back!" Ava pushed in front of her brother.

"How much room do you need?"

"What do you think she'll look like?" Ava peered out the window.

"A girl."

They hushed as a gray Nash 600 sedan came to a stop in front of their house. James's car door began to open, but the passenger door opened first and out jumped a young woman. To Ava's amazement, the girl ran to Victoria and embraced her without restraint. Ava tried to get a clear image of her from behind Victoria as Ella began to cry.

"Don't you need to check on Ella?" Carson asked.

"You are just as much her uncle as I am her aunt."

Victoria and now Sheffield were still blocking their view, so Ava relented and went to see about her niece.

"What's wrong, Ella?"

The toddler had dropped the pot and was holding up her finger to be seen.

"Did you pinch your finger?"

Ava scooped her up, examined the extended finger, which was a little purple, and kissed it.

"All better now," she said, thinking of how her niece's life was about to be turned upside down. Today, she got a new mother. Ava suddenly ached for Estelle, wishing once again that her sister-in-law had not died and was able to raise the baby she had so longed for.

Ella was still sobbing when Ava heard the front door opening behind them.

"Shh, Shh," she continued to comfort, smoothing down Ella's yellow dress. She knew her mother wouldn't want Ella crying at such an important meeting.

"What's wrong with her?" Victoria was now by her side.

"She just pinched her finger," Ava said turning with Ella in her arms, and as she did, the little girl caught sight of her father and the woman by his side. Her crying paused, and her amber eyes stared at the strangers. She had only seen her father once before and didn't remember him.

"Come here. Let me see that finger." The woman moved forward and took Ella from Ava's arms.

Now Ava could see her brother's wife. She was blond and attractive with curly, short hair, blue eyes, and a sporty but feminine figure in a peach dress.

"What a pretty little finger! Let's see if we can wiggle it." The woman moved Ella's finger back and forth and laughed out loud when the child began wiggling it herself. "It's perfect!"

"James can you introduce your wife to your sister and your brother?" Victoria asked now that Ella was settled.

"This is Vivie Crowder. I mean Vivie Stilwell. We just got married last weekend." He grinned at his blunder. "Vivie, this is my sister Ava and my brother Carson.

"It was two weekends ago," Vivie corrected with another loud cackle, kissing him on the cheek.

Ava blushed at her show of affection in front of their parents. James also blushed, but it was good to see color again in his face. The last time Ava had seen him was not long after he had learned of Estelle's death and returned from the war, and he was thin and pale and unable to come home or even look at Ella for his grief.

"I've heard so much about you all, and it's simply wonderful to finally meet you." Vivie hugged Carson and then Ava with one arm as she held Ella with the other.

"I'm afraid we've heard very little about you," Victoria said what they were all thinking. "So, we can't wait to learn everything about you!"

"Oh bananas, where do I start? James you should write more in your letters."

"Amen," Victoria agreed.

"We have all evening to talk," Sheffield joined in, putting a calming hand on his wife's back. One day had not been enough to prepare them for the sudden change in their lives. Before yesterday, they didn't even know that their son had been seeing a woman again.

"Ella, I bet you can't wait to see your daddy!" Vivie handed the child to her father, and the whole family held their breath.

James's body stiffened as he held the little girl like a box of breakables.

"Hi there," he said, and Ella looked up at him.

For a moment, Ava thought James's composure would break. Ella did have the same eyes and high cheekbones as her mother. A slight quiver moved over his lips before he smiled at his daughter.

"James, you have something for her, remember?" Vivie reminded.

"Oh, yes." James handed the girl back to her new mother and opened up their suitcase. Out of it, came the prettiest doll Ava had ever seen. She had soft brown hair, brown eyes, and a lacey white dress with a matching bonnet.

Ella's eyes widened as she took the doll.

"Dah! Dah! Dah!" Ella squealed.

"What does that mean?" Grandpa Chester asked from where he now sat in his rocking chair observing them all.

"She is trying to say doll," Victoria answered him, and he grunted. Babies never made sense to him.

4

"I'm sure you are both tired and worn out from your trip. Why don't you rest a little while Ava and I cook dinner," Victoria said.

Ava sighed. Now that she was a married woman, her mother expected her to do more and more of her share of the family cooking, and she was tired of it.

"Nonsense, I've been sitting in a car all afternoon. Let me help too!" Vivie offered.

Victoria tried to smile, not sure if she was ready to share her kitchen with a woman they had just met.

"Very well. Just let Ella play with her new doll in here with the men, and we'll get started."

Sheffield turned on the radio, and news from the Nuremberg trial filled the room. Ava followed her mother and Vivie, glad for once to be in the kitchen!

"I'll start on the fried chicken. Ava, you start on the biscuits, and Vivie, why don't..."

"Oh, can I make the biscuits?" Vivie interrupted. "That is one thing I'm good at."

"I...I suppose." Victoria's dark eyebrows arched, and Ava knew her mother was not pleased. She had a certain way she liked her biscuits made, and she had taught Ava precisely how to make them.

"Ava, get her out the flour, lard, buttermilk, and the iron skillet. Then, get to cutting up the potatoes."

"So, how did you and James meet?" Ava asked the question she had been waiting to ask ever since the letter had arrived. Victoria didn't remonstrate, and Ava knew that her mother wanted to know just as much. James would barely tell them anything.

"What a story!" Vivie laughed. She had the loudest, shrillest laugh for a woman that Ava had ever heard. "We met two months ago."

"Goodness, two whole months ago!" Victoria exclaimed. When it came to her children, she couldn't help but speak her mind.

"I know it seems sudden, but we were instantly in love. I can't explain it."

This time Victoria said nothing.

"I think that's romantic," Ava said, but it was still hard to imagine her brother in love with anyone other than Estelle. Theirs was a different story. They had known and loved each other since they were children.

"I was seeing one of James's friends from the airport, and he had invited me and Elijah to visit him at work. Elijah's my youngest brother. He's six and fascinated with anything loud and anything that goes up in the air. We were playing Mother May I while waiting for another plane to take off when James came walking by with a cart of luggage. I saw him watching us and smiled. The next time he came by, I had just told Elijah to take five giant steps forward. James looked both ways and out stepped him all the way to where I was standing! Elijah thought it was the funniest thing he had ever seen, and that is when I fell in love with James."

She paused in her story, and Ava could just picture her brother doing exactly as she had described. It was the old James, the James before the war.

"Ava, chop while you listen!" Victoria said.

"Yes, mother. What happened after that?"

"He asked me out the very same afternoon. His friend George was furious, but James claimed he thought I was

6

George's sister. He still sticks by his story, but I don't believe him! I fixed George up with a friend of mine and went out with James that night. Do you have a biscuit cutter?"

"Whatever do you need one of those for?" Victoria said as fresh chicken began popping in the skillet in front of her.

"To cut the biscuits with. My grandmother always liked to make sure that everyone got the same size biscuit."

"Nonsense, just pinch off the dough and roll it with your hands." Victoria continued with her chicken.

"I'll give it a try." Vivie put her hands back in the dough. "Ava, where is your husband, Edwin, I believe?"

"I'll go check on him! He should have been back from work by now."

"Ava, I was really hoping you would cook the peas while I fry up the potatoes. I think Edwin knows the way to our house."

"Mrs. Stilwell, I can do the peas too. Ava can go."
Victoria sighed.

"Alright, but Ava, be quick, and Vivie, call me Victoria. We are not formal in this family."

Ava ran the short distance between their two houses. The newly installed porch light was on, which meant Edwin was home. Electricity had come to their area over the summer, and she was still getting used to the unfamiliar lights.

"Edwin!" she called as the front door pounded open behind her.

"In here," he called back.

She found him in their bedroom, scrubbing his face and hands with a wet rag, the freshly ironed white shirt she had laid out for him still on the bed.

"What's taking so long?"

"Trying to get all this grime off for your family. Your parents won't like it if I show up with soot from the furnace all over me."

"Here, let me see." Ava took the rag from him and turned his head to the side with her finger. She loved the way his skin felt just after a shave. There was still a resilient black smudge behind his cheek bone. It was the burn below it, though, that caught her eye, and she ran her finger gingerly over it.

"Did you get burned today?"

"Just a little." He winced and took her hand away from his face.

"I'm sick of this! It feels like you're in combat again, and I have to worry about whether or not you're going to come home in one piece every day!

"Let's not fight tonight, Songbird." Edwin pulled her to him and kissed her, and she let her anger go.

It was hard to stay mad at him when he called her by the nickname he had given her before they were married. He seldom used it, but when he did, she felt his love. She wanted to keep kissing him, but remembered that her mother was waiting for them.

"Mom needs me back in the kitchen. Let's go!"

He pulled away from her and began to put on the clean shirt. Good food and hard labor had made him fuller and more muscular now than when he had first come home from the war.

"Do you like your new sister-in-law?" he asked.

"Vivie is great, I think. I don't know if Mom thinks so yet. She lectured me and Carson about overwhelming her all afternoon, but I think Mom is the only one being overwhelmed!"

Ava grabbed his hand and began pulling him toward the door. She didn't want to miss anymore of the drama between Vivie and her mother.

"You know, Vivie can't be any older than me. She looks really young and has the most unusual laugh."

"If James loves her, I am sure everyone will love her in time," Edwin said and then laughed himself, trying to keep up with his wife.

The Stilwell family had been gracious to him and given him a new family when he needed one. For that, he would ever be grateful.

"Lord, bless this food that we are about to partake of, and thank you for the hands that have prepared it. We also thank you for bringing our son safely through the war and home at last with his new wife, Vivie. Bless them as they build a new life together. Amen," Sheffield spoke over the now completed dinner.

"Amen," Grandpa Chester seconded and began helping himself to the largest chicken leg on the platter.

"Ella, come to Grammy. It's time to eat," Victoria called to the child who now had her new doll sitting in the cooking pot as she pulled it across the floor.

"I'll feed her, Mrs. Stilwell, I mean Victoria. You must be so tired from cooking this feast. You barely let anyone else do anything." Vivie took the child in her arms.

9

"You don't have to do that. I'm used to it."

"Mom, Vivie is also used to feeding children. Please let her do it," James said, watching his wife with his daughter.

"Alright, if you both insist." Victoria sat down next to her husband. It felt odd having an empty lap at the dinner table. For two years she had fed and cared for Ella, and it seemed strange to be watching her from across the table.

"Yes, with three younger brothers, I have had my fair share of feeding children." Vivie laughed and offered Ella a bite of potato.

"Make sure she eats her purple hull peas. She tries to turn her nose up at them," Victoria said.

"James said you worked during the war at the Bell Bomber plant in Marietta, GA," Carson spoke up. He loved his niece but didn't want to talk about what she was or was not eating all evening.

"You are looking at a real-life Rosie the Riveter and welder!" Tied back hair, slacks, muscles, and all!"

"Didn't you hate pulling your hair up every day?" Ava asked.

"That's why I cut it off. Easier and safer that way. My hair used to be long like yours."

"Smart girl," Grandpa Chester said. "Read in the paper about a girl in Illinois who got her hair tangled up in a bit shaft and lost part of her scalp."

Ava shuddered. That was not what she wanted to hear about while she ate her dinner.

"Your plant made the big B-29s for the Army, right?" Sheffield now asked.

"Hundreds of them. Most were used in the Pacific."

"Did you enjoy working in a factory?" Ava asked next.

10

"I truly did and was sad when the plant closed."

"Why did it close?"

"With the war over, there isn't as much of a need for long-range bombers anymore," Sheffield answered for his daughter-in-law.

"Still seems a shame that all those people lost their jobs," Ava said.

"Let's just be thankful the war is over!" Victoria threw up her hands.

"Did you make good money?" Carson asked between bites of biscuit, noticing something different about them.

"Carson Stilwell, have you forgotten your manners!" Victoria gave him a stern look. "We don't ask people about their money."

"What? She's family now. We can be honest with family."

Vivie laughed her loudest laugh yet, and Ava could have sworn the table shook with it.

"Worked sixty hours a week most weeks. See that car out there? Saved up and bought it all by myself."

The idea of a woman owning her own car pleased Ava, and she recalled the first paycheck she earned from Wakefield's Department Store and the way it made her feel.

"So, don't worry Carson. You and dad can keep my old car. I'm sure preachers don't' make much money anyways." James grinned, still finding it hard to believe that his younger brother became a preacher while he was away in the war.

"That is very generous of you," Carson said.

"Edwin, you're awfully quiet tonight. Are you feeling alright?" Victoria noticed her silent son-in-law on the far side of the table.

11

"Yes, ma'am, just tired from working all day."

"Do you usually work on Saturdays?" Vivie asked.

"Only on occasion," he replied. "At the bomber plant, was the work hard to learn?" Listening to their conversation, he just couldn't picture a woman welding or working as a molder in a pipe shop like him. He wouldn't say it out loud, but it seemed far too dangerous and difficult. He would never want Ava working that way.

"At first, it was hard. But after you do something a thousand times, it becomes kind of natural like."

"Ella, I see you over there not eating your peas. I want to see them all gone," Victoria spoke to her granddaughter.

"Let's not forget these peas." Vivie scooped them up and held the spoon out for Ella, but when the little girl still refused them, she put them in her own mouth instead. "There, the peas are gone!" Ella giggled, and Vivie hugged her.

"Well, I declare," Victoria said, and everyone but she laughed.

"Sorry, Mrs. Stilwell, I mean Victoria. I'll do a better job feeding her next time."

"Speaking of next time, Mom and Dad, Vivie and I have decided that before we take Ella home to live with us next weekend, she should be more used to Vivie. So, we thought Vivie could stay the week with you while I go back to Atlanta to work."

"Good idea, son," Sheffield said as his wife struggled for words for once. "It will also give us more time to get acquainted with our new daughter-in-law."

Victoria just smiled, but Ava could see the real meaning behind it. Her mother had a hard enough time sharing her kitchen with a stranger, much less her home and granddaughter!

Later that evening when everyone grew as tired as Edwin, James caught his sister alone for a few seconds on the front porch.

"Look after Vivie this week for me," he said, and the request reminded Ava of a similar request he had made of her a few years ago when he left Estelle behind for the Army.

"Afraid Mom might be too much for her?" Ava laughed.

"Or the other way around." He laughed too, but a sudden crease came over his forehead, and he ran a hand unconsciously through his black hair.

"Do you want to come see what I've done with the house?" Ava asked and then immediately wished she hadn't when the crease deepened.

"Ava, I'm sorry, but I don't think I can ever step through that front door again."

"No, I'm sorry, I should have…"

"No need to apologize. Go make new memories there for me. Ok?"

He was smiling again, and Ava hugged him.

"Glad to have you back."

Edwin came out the door, and they told James good night. It felt odd walking from her old house to James's old house. Everything was upside down. James and his new wife were sleeping tonight in her old room, and she and Edwin were sleeping in the house her brother knew before the war and before everything changed.

Chapter 2

Ava stared at the Wakefield's Department Store window display. It was obvious that the war was over. No more flags affixed throughout it, and no more drab-colored suits. Instead, it was full of rich fall colors. The mannequins wore orange, yellow, and maroon dresses, but it was their matching hats that drew the eye.

"Are you coming in?" Rosemary opened the door to the department store and asked her cousin. It was late Wednesday morning, and they had few shoppers at the moment.

"You have new hats." Ava followed her through the door and into her old place of employment.

"Hundreds of them. Need a new one?"

"I think I'll surprise Edwin with one."

"Ava, good to see you back in the store, dear!" Lorraine Crocket, the store manager, called from behind the hosiery counter. "How are your studies coming along?"

"Good, thank you for asking. I'm almost halfway through."

"My how time flies!"

The door opened again behind them, and a well-dressed woman walked in.

"Hello, Mrs. Treadway. Is there anything either myself or one of our ladies can do you for you today?" Mrs. Crockett greeted with the warm smile she reserved for their best customers.

Rosemary waved to Ava from a rack of women's hats, and Ava went to her.

"This one would look nice with your yellow dress." Rosemary placed a yellow hat with black lace on Ava's head and held a mirror up for her to look into.

"Aren't you the salesman now," Ava said as she admired the hat on her head. It was just the right size, not too large and not too small. It also contrasted well with her dark hair.

"I don't get to sale things very often now that Mrs. Crockett has made me the cashier."

"Don't you like handling all the money?"

"As long as it balances out right each night. I have to be so careful that sometimes it makes me nervous."

"You were always better at math than me. I'll take the hat." Ava pulled the hat off her head and handed it back to her cousin.

Rosemary smiled. She might not have finished high school and moved on to college like her cousin, but she had learned and grew in other ways. Of all the employees at the store, she felt that Mrs. Crockett trusted her most.

"Come on. Let's get your hat and get out of here. I'm starving."

Ava followed Rosemary to the cashier's desk and waited while she filled out her ticket. She heard whistling and turned to see Douglas, a black, middle-aged man and her former co-worker, putting out men's dress shoes at the other end of the store.

"Is Douglas allowed in the store during open hours?" Ava tried to whisper but failed.

"Yes," Rosemary actually did whisper, "Mrs. Crockett has made up her mind that she doesn't care anymore what people like Geraldine Dallas say. He's the best stocker this store has ever had."

"I was so afraid they would let him go after the war," Ava said.

"Me too."

Douglas noticed Ava and waved, and Ava walked over to him.

"Good to see you, Douglas."

"You too. Pretty as ever. Haven't stopped singing now, have you?"

"Heaven's no! I'm actually going to band practice right after I have lunch with Rosemary."

"Never stop. It makes life sweeter." He smiled and told her goodbye before going to the back for more shoes.

Ava thought about his advice as she and Rosemary left the store. If anything, she was singing now more than ever. Between her music classes at Jacksonville State Teachers College, the band, and church, she felt that she was singing all the time. Was her life sweeter? Yes, it was, but she blamed Edwin for that, not her music.

"Are you coming to see me and the band at Fort McClellan Saturday night with Edwin and James and Vivie?"

Rosemary sighed as she and Ava moved over on the sidewalk to make room for a woman with her two boys passing. Noble Street was suddenly more crowded now that lunch time was approaching.

"Mom, can we have some licorice for dessert?" the tallest boy asked his mother.

"We'll see," the mother replied.

"I don't know," Rosemary said once they were side by side again.

"Well, why wouldn't you?"

"I don't know if I can ever go back to that fort."

"Rosemary, let the past be the past. You can make new memories there now." Ava smiled, realizing she was repeating her brother. "Didn't you say Jake was coming into town and wanted to see you?"

"Yes, he's coming home," Rosemary answered, and a frown furrowed her face. "You know, maybe we will go."

The thought of being alone with Jake was worse somehow than the thought of being where she had met the man who had betrayed her.

"Yay! You won't be sorry! It will be so much fun to dance and to see James happy again!"

"How are things going with Vivie?"

"When I stop by, she's either playing on the floor with Ella or following Mom around laughing about something, which Mom doesn't seem to find funny."

"Sounds like Ella has fallen in love with her. My parents already think a lot of her too."

"Everyone does, except my mom."

Ava's stomach growled, and she was glad they were now at the Palace Drug Store.

When Ava arrived at band practice, many of the musicians were already warming up. Saxophones, trumpets, violins, double basses, and drums were all noisily preparing themselves for the music ahead. Ava recognized many faces but also saw some she had never seen before. That is how it was at every practice. With the war over, men who had been playing for Uncle Sam were now back in the band. Some, however, like the famous band leader Glenn Miller, never returned, their music lost forever with the war.

"Hi Ava," a trumpeter called out between puffs on his instrument.

"Hi Jonathan."

"Ava, I have a new one for you," Willie Harold, the slender band leader, appeared with a sheet of music. "I know it is short work, but we're going to perform it Saturday night for the boys. It's popular on the charts, and I think it would go over well with our crowd. I know you can sing it just as good as Betty Hutton."

"I'll try," Ava said.

Willie smiled at her and took his spot in front of the semicircle of musicians.

"Ok, let's play," he spoke, his voice suddenly growing.

There was silence, then the soft tap of Willie's baton, and then the ripple and boom of the many harmonizing instruments. The music always rushed through Ava's soul and brought her alive no matter how tired she was. She almost forgot to look at the sheet music in her hands to see when her part was. Looking at it now, she read "Doctor, Lawyer, Indian Chief" and recognized it. A minute later, she was singing with the band.

"There's a doctor livin' in your town. There's a lawyer and an Indian too. And neither doctor, lawyer nor Injun chief could love you anymore than I do."

18

"There's a barrel of fish in the ocean," Ava sang as she mixed together peanut butter, flour, an egg, and butter. "There's a lot of little birds in the blue."

She stopped stirring and stopped her song at the same time.

"Let's see. That leaves only sugar." She measured out a cup of sugar and added it to her mixture. "There," she said and held up her hand counting off each of the five ingredients with her fingers.

She now began to pinch off the dough and roll it into palm-size balls.

"And neither fish nor fowl says the wise old owl can you love you anymore than I do," she sang again, determined to both make good cookies and remember all the words to her latest song.

"Ava, you ready for me?" Vivie called through the front door.

Ava rinsed off her hands and ran to let her in.

"Yes, yes, come in."

"What an adorable house!" Vivie said, walking around the living room and taking it all in.

Ava followed her eyes from the sofa, to James's old arm chair, to the pictures and little basket of dried flowers sitting between them.

"I try to keep it clean," Ava said, noticing one of Edwin's dirty socks behind the chair. She picked it up and tossed it in a basket just inside their bedroom door.

"Edwin is always taking his socks off when he comes home from work, and they end up wherever he lands."

Vivie laughed. She was holding the picture taken of James in his military uniform just before he left for Europe.

19

"I will always love that picture of him." Ava looked at it with her. James smiled up at them both, clean shaven and ready for anything the war had in store for him.

"He's very handsome in it. So, this is how he was before the war," Vivie said, and she sat the picture back down on the table next to Edwin's service picture and a picture of Edwin and Ava right after they were married.

She glanced back around the room as if looking for other old signs of James, and Ava suddenly realized that it must be strange to be in a house that your husband once shared with another woman.

"Want to come to the kitchen? I'm making us some cookies."

"I'll go anywhere for cookies!" Vivie laughed, and the curls surrounding her head bounced.

"I was always taught to offer food when having visitors," Ava said, putting her hands back in the cookie dough.

"I like that rule!" Vivie sat down at the kitchen table. "Thanks for having me over this afternoon. I know your mother could use a break from me."

"I'm glad you came." Ava's grey eyes widened at her sister-in-law's quick understanding of her mother.

"Bananas! I would need a break from me too if I was her." Vivie laughed, so Ava did too. "You know your mother works harder than any woman I have ever seen. With all the washing, cooking, gardening, helping out your dad when she can, and taking care of Ella, I don't see how she just doesn't fall over."

"Unfortunately, my mother does not believe in rest," Ava said. "The only time I have ever seen her lie down is when she sleeping or sick."

Ava slid the cookie pan in the oven and sat down next to Vivie.

"Will you tell me about Estelle?" Vivie asked, and Ava stared back at her, unsure if she should.

"Seriously, I would love to hear about her. After all, I will be raising her daughter, and I want to know what kind of person she was. James refuses to talk about her."

"Well," Ava started and stopped, grief gripping her own heart even now. "She was the kindest person I have ever known, putting everyone before herself. Everybody loved her. She treated me like one of her own sisters." Ava stopped again, afraid she was telling too much.

"No, go on," Vivie pleaded.

"She couldn't stand the thought of being separated from James when he left for the war. She even followed him to basic training in Texas. If she wouldn't have gotten so sick with her pregnancy, she might have followed him to Europe." Ava smiled now as she remembered.

"James really loved her."

"He did, and he loves you now."

"Not like that," Vivie said and then laughed at the look Ava gave her. "It's ok to be honest."

"But I'm sure he loves you. I mean to have married you after so little time." Ava cringed, wishing she could take back her last words.

"Oh, he thinks he loves me, but he doesn't really love me yet. I love him. I did from the moment I saw him. He loves the way I make him feel, though. He told me that when he is with me he feels alive again, and I'm glad. He also wants a mother for Ella and thinks I would be a good one."

21

This time Ava said nothing. She didn't know what to say as new realizations entered her mind. Her brother would only come for Ella when he was married again and had a mother for his daughter. That is why he had stayed away for so long, and she felt sorry for having been angry at him.

"Ella thinks the world of you," Ava finally said.

"And I think the world of her."

The smell of cookies pulled Ava away from her thoughts, and she got a dish towel and pulled the pan out of the oven.

"These look delicious," Vivie said.

"Give them a couple of minutes, and we'll eat them warm but not too crumbly. They're actually a recipe Edwin taught me, his grandmother's peanut butter cookies by hand recipe. Who knew men could cook!"

"Not James!" Vivie laughed.

"I know you two will be happy," Ava said, hoping that what she was saying was true and that James hadn't made a mistake for Ella's sake.

"We already are." Vivie smiled. "And don't worry, he will love me!"

Ava laughed first this time. She really did like her new sister-in-law.

"Now, tell me about your band."

Ava told her about the band and how Rosemary and Jake were going to the dance with them as they ate half a plate of cookies together. It was good to talk and laugh with another woman her age in the little house again.

Chapter 3

"And, confidentially, I confess. I sent a note to the local press," Ava sang out over the big band. "That I'll be changing my home address for you, follow through."

She remembered all the words, and they flowed out effortlessly now. The song was light and carefree, matching the mood at the fort. Uniformed men were dancing and laughing throughout the room. These men had arrived at the end. They were in training for occupational duty now, not war.

"Tell the doctor to stick to his practice. Tell the lawyer to settle his case. Send the Injun chief and his tommy hawk back to little Rain-in-the-Face!"

As she continued to sing, her eyes sought Edwin. He was standing in the back, gazing up at her with the intense blue eyes that always made her feel as though he could see even her thoughts. He loved her best when she was singing, and she sang for him.

"Cause you know, know, know it couldn't be true. That anyone else could love you like I do."

She now saw James and Vivie a little ways from where Edwin stood. Their faces were red from dancing as James first swung Vivie out and then pulled her back to him. She and Vivie had begged James to wear his dress uniform, but he refused, saying that "over two years of that get-up was more than enough." He looked nice, however, in pleated, khaki pants and a white button-up shirt with rolled-up sleeves.

Not far from them, Jake and Rosemary were also dancing. Rosemary was smiling, but Ava still noticed a hint of sadness behind her hazel eyes, which were greener tonight next to her teal wrap dress. She wondered if Jake noticed too. She couldn't help but remember the first time she sang at the fort. Rosemary had been reluctantly brought to accompany her, and Lieutenant Percy Bledsoe had coerced Rosemary into dancing with him and later into giving him her heart before she realized he was a married man. Ava shuddered remembering the night Rosemary had discovered the truth and made her promise to never tell anyone. Jake knew the truth but loved her anyway. He had forgiven her, but she had still not forgiven herself.

"Like I do, like I do," Ava finished the song and turned her eyes back upon Edwin. Couples stopped dancing and clapped for her before the band began playing Benny Goodman's "Sing, Sing, Sing" without her.

She made her way through the crowded floor to where Edwin, James, and Vivie stood waiting for her.

"Not bad, sis. Mom was right." James put an arm around her. "You sound different with the band."

"How so?"

"More grown-up like. Like a real big band singer."

"She is a real big band singer, you goof," Vivie said.

"I still prefer to sing with you and Carson and your banjos." Ava laughed.

"I haven't heard this banjo playing you all talk about yet." Vivie turned down her bottom lip in a pout.

"We'll have to fix that when we get home!"

"If you get Mom started, we'll be up all night," James said.

"Who cares! You're leaving tomorrow, and Edwin didn't have to work today. Let's stay up all night!"

"Ava, loved hearing you sing again," Jake said as he and Rosemary joined their group. "Last time I heard you sing was at that ridiculous party my mom gave before I left for the Navy."

"A little different here?"

"A little." Jake laughed.

"Next time we hear her sing, she'll be performing with the Tommy Dorsey band," James said.

"I think I'm a far cry from that!"

"What do you think about Fort McClellan? Does it live up to Navy standards?" Edwin asked Jake. Coming back to the fort where he spent weeks in infantry replacement training felt like an odd homecoming without all the familiar faces.

"These boys have got it lucky," Jake replied, "I don't think they'll get much farther than here. My father was told that even occupational training is about to end."

"Would they close the fort then?" Rosemary asked.

"Don't know."

"All right, Vivie and I are dancing," James announced and pulled his wife back out on the dance floor.

"Come on, Edwin. I'm tired of watching other people dance."

Ava and Edwin followed James and Vivie onto the dance floor, and Jake and Rosemary did the same. Moving to the music with Edwin's arms around her made Ava light-headed, and she vowed to always remember the moment. They had each other and were dancing. James was happy again and dancing with his new wife, and Rosemary she believed was on her way back to happiness. What more could she ask for?

"Sydney loved dancing here," Edwin said in her ear over the music.

Just like that the joy of the moment left her, and she could feel the blood draining from her face as she also now thought of Edwin's comrade and friend. She herself had danced with Sydney right here in this room. He was the best dancer she had ever partnered with. Sydney Saunders and Barry Roosevelt were Edwin's closest friends in the Army, and both died during the war. She wondered how many other men had their last dance on this floor.

"I'm sorry, Ava." Edwin held her closer. "I shouldn't have mentioned him. I know you want us all to be happy tonight. It's just hard not to remember."

"And you shouldn't stop. We must always remember them."

Ava held him closer, as well, moving slowly now to the swelling music, thanking God again for bringing him home to her. He winced involuntarily, and she knew she must have touched another place he had been burned at the pipe shop.

"Edwin!" She jerked away from him, but he pulled her back and kissed her quickly before she could say anything more.

She smiled up at him, her ruby lips standing out even in the dimly-lit room, and the worry over his burns left her as he began spinning her around to the drum solo.

Ava held Ella tightly in her arms as Carson and James played their banjos, her mother played the piano, and her father sang. She was done with singing. All she wanted to do now was listen to her family while she held Ella. Tomorrow Ella would be leaving, and she would be losing the last piece of Estelle that was left to them. At first, she had avoided the little girl, angry that her sister-in-law had died at a time when she shouldn't have. Now, she clung to her, loving her gentle, playful spirit. She ran her fingers through her fine hair as she slept in her lap. It was close to two o'clock in the morning and way past the child's bedtime.

"Cause some morning yonder I'm gonna sit down by your side," Sheffield sang out as if he were leading the music in their church instead of sitting in his living room. "They'll never be another tear to run down from my eyes."

"Amen," Grandpa Chester mumbled from his rocking chair before drifting back off to sleep. Ava laughed. Her grandfather probably thought they were in church.

"And there we'll talk things over like we never have before," Sheffield continued.

For once, Ava didn't mind that all their songs seemed to be about heaven. She did have a lot of questions for God, and at least in heaven, she would never have to tell someone she loved goodbye again.

"I don't see how she sleeps through all of this." Vivie leaned over and rubbed Ella's arm, which didn't move.

"She's been sleeping through Mom's late night singings since she was an infant. That's how."

"Life is about to be much different for her, but I will make it as happy and fun as I possibly can," Vivie vowed.

Ava smiled at her, fighting back the tears she knew would be harder to fight back tomorrow.

"Cause some morning yonder I'm gonna sit down by your side," the chorus began again. This time Victoria joined in, her rich, alto voice blending perfectly with her husband's tenor.

Ava watched her mother. Like herself, she was her best when she was performing. Her pale blue eyes and face shone as she sang each word, her fingers alighting on the piano keys without effort. She needed no sheet music, the notes were written in her head and in her heart.

The chorus and song ended, and only then could Ava hear Edwin snoring from where he lay behind her.

"I'm surprised, James," Carson said, "I didn't think you would be able to play a lick after being without your banjo for so long.

"To be honest, me either. I guess there are just some things you never forget."

"It's all in the teaching." Sheffield patted his oldest son on the back.

"Oh, James, bring the banjo home with us!" Vivie pleaded.

"I think it needs to stay where it belongs."

"It belongs with you," Victoria joined in.

"You can play it for me and Ella. It will remind her of her first home."

"It's staying here." He stood up and laid the banjo down. "It's late. Why don't we all get some rest now? Shouldn't she be in her bed?" He pointed at Ella.

"She's perfectly fine with Ava," Victoria said.

"We quitting?" Sheffield asked.

"Thought we were just warming up?" Carson said.

"I have to drive home tomorrow afternoon, and you have to preach. I think it's time."

"Time for what?" Edwin woke up.

"I think you've already gone to bed." Ava laughed.

Vivie laughed too, but it was hollow sounding compared to her usual laugh, and Ava noticed that her face looked pinched, like she would rather scream or cry.

"Here, I'll take Ella." Victoria was now standing over them, and Ava lifted up the child to her.

Ella's eyes opened, and she let out a soft cry.

"James, do you want to tell her goodnight?"

"Good night, I'll see you all in the morning," he said and disappeared into Ava's old bedroom.

"Here, I'll tell her goodnight." Vivie stood up and kissed Ella on the cheek. "Goodnight, sweet princess."

"You're going to make a good mother for her," Victoria said.

"I will do all I possibly can for her."

"I know, and don't you worry, I'll get that banjo in that car with you if it's the last thing I do."

Vivie smiled at her mother-in-law. Maybe they understood each other after all.

They all said their goodnights and left Grandpa Chester asleep in his chair.

The night went by quickly, but the church service was long. Edwin kept elbowing Ava to keep her awake. She couldn't wait for late afternoon when she could lay down for one of Grandpa Chester's Sunday afternoon naps. After church, Rosemary, her parents, Jude and Myrtle, and her sister, Judith, came over for Sunday lunch. Carson had left early that morning to preach at his church in Heflin. The dishes were all emptied and put away, and they all sat talking in the living room after stuffing themselves with cube steak and gravy.

"Careful with Ella," Myrtle chided her seven year-old daughter.

"But Mom, she likes it," Judith called out as she swung Ella around yet again.

Ella squealed, agreeing with her older cousin.

"I said that's enough. You're going to make her lose her lunch."

The girls gave in and collapsed together in a laughing pile on the floor.

"They do have fun together." Vivie cackled as loud as the little ones.

"That they do." Sheffield also laughed and joined them on the floor. Everyone but James laughed now as his father tickled the two girls.

"Stop! Stop!" Judith shouted. She was older now and not quite as chubby as she once was, but her still plump cheeks were bright red from laughing so hard.

"They may both lose their lunches now," Victoria said.

"Wait till Ella meets my brothers," Vivie said. "They tickle with no mercy."

"That's the best kind of brothers." Jude chuckled.

"I don't know about that," Ava disagreed, looking at her silent brother who sat watching the girls with little expression. "James and Carson could be downright mean!"

"Me, mean?" James smiled now, and she was glad of it. "Never."

"You'll have to bring Ella back often to visit. Judith will miss her so," Myrtle said.

"We all will," Rosemary added.

"Of course," Vivie assured. "And you all feel free to come visit us in Atlanta too."

"Speaking of." James stood up. "I think it's time we get on the road."

"Do you really have to?" Victoria also stood up, wishing she could will her son to stay put a while longer.

"I didn't think you wanted us on the road after dark."

"I guess not. Let me get Ella's things."

"I'll help you load up," Edwin offered.

"Me too." Sheffield groaned as he stood up and stretched out his long legs. "I'm getting too old to wallow on the floor."

"No! No!" Ella giggled, trying to pull her grandfather back down on the floor as the screen door opened.

"You mean I didn't stay gone long enough to miss you leaving," Carson greeted his brother.

"Not this time." James laughed. "You get to see my ugly face again."

"Aw, well at least Vivie has a pretty face."

"Thanks Carson," Vivie said. "Now, you can say goodbye to Ella too."

"That may be more difficult to do," Carson admitted, and Ava could already feel tears pooling at the back of her eyes.

"You hungry? Mom left a plate for you on the table," Ava said to him.

"Not yet. The Faulkners made me eat a little lunch with them before I left." He took off his jacket and tie and hung them on the back of one of the kitchen chairs that had been slid into the living room.

"Did you give them a good sermon this morning?" Sheffield asked.

"The best." Carson grinned.

31

"Sheffield, please go wake up my father," Victoria called to her husband. "He shouldn't miss this, nap or no nap."

"All right, but he won't be happy." Sheffield went back to Grandpa Chester's room.

Soon the packing was complete, and they were all standing outside as the men loaded the car. Ella had been transferred from Jude to Myrtle and Judith to Rosemary to Ava as they each wanted to hold the little girl one last time before she left them.

"Sing all those songs I taught you to your daddy and Vivie, ok," Ava told her, and Ella nodded her head, trying to figure out what was happening to them all.

"Mom, what's in this box?" James asked and then grunted again as he lifted the long, rectangular trunk into the back of the car.

"Just some of Ella's toys and some sewing stuff I promised Vivie." Victoria winked at her daughter-in-law.

"I didn't realize that little girls came with so much."

"Of course they do," Vivie said.

"Annie, let me see her," Grandpa Chester spoke to Ava, calling her the name he had called her since she was born and decided that he didn't like the name she was given.

Ava kissed Ella on the cheek and handed her to her grandfather.

"Be a good little bunny for Grandpa," he said, kissing her as well.

"My turn." Victoria held out her hands, and Ella went to her.

"I love you and will see you soon, my sweet girl." Victoria held the little girl to her chest. "Love your daddy and your new mother, because they do love you." She clung to the child a few moments longer and then called to her husband who took Ella from her.

Victoria walked over to her oldest son and hugged him next, and the tears she had held at bay for Ella came streaming down her cheeks. Ava started to cry too, and Edwin put his arm around her.

"We'll go visit them," he whispered in her ear, and she laid her head on his arm.

"Night, night, Ella." Carson patted Ella on the head. It was what he told her every night. She looked up at her uncle and grinned.

"We all love you," Sheffield said and kissed his granddaughter.

They finished their goodbyes, and Vivie put Ella in the car between herself and James.

"Bye, Ella!" Judith shouted as they drove away.

Chapter 4

With Ella now gone, Victoria did what she always did when life was difficult for her. She threw herself into a project and worked herself to distraction. When James left for the war, she changed the Four Mile Community Garden Club to the Women Advancing the War Efforts Committee and did all she could from the home front to bring her son back. Now, with the war over and more time on her hands without Ella, she decided to regroup the garden club. Besides music, there was nothing she loved more than flowers. In the two weeks after James, Vivie, and her granddaughter left, she studied her indoor cacti, fastidiously cleaned every corner of the house, and baked pound cakes. She wanted the first meeting back to be better than any the ladies could remember.

"Welcome back to our garden club. I hope you all have fun and learn a little bit from each other," Victoria said when all of the chairs were full. "It's so good to have most of us back and to see a new face too." She nodded at Floraline Gunter, Estelle's younger sister and Ava's former school friend.

Ava smiled at Floraline who wiggled in her chair at being singled out. Now, that Floraline was a housewife and a mother-to-be, she had made Victoria's invite list, and Ava was relieved to have someone else her age there.

"With winter approaching, Myrtle and I thought that caring for our indoor cacti would make a good topic of discussion. That is why I asked you all to bring one if you could. When Ava calls out your name, please respond and tell us what kind of cactus you brought along."

Victoria now nodded at her daughter, and Ava began calling out names from the alphabetical list.

"Myrtle Bonds."

"Present," Myrtle said, followed by the nervous giggle which always came when she was the center of attention. "I brought a pincushion cactus."

Ava placed a check by her name and moved on.

"Ingrid Carson."

"My sister-in-law is sick with the crud and had to miss today," Victoria said.

"What a shame." Maris Ingram sighed, and Victoria did as well. If anyone needed help with their flowers, it was Ingrid.

"Abigail Dempsey."

"Present," Abigail answered. "I brought the Christmas cactus my grandmother passed down to me."

She held up the cactus, proud of the pink and white buds emerging even before November.

"What lovely little buds," Delores Waters complimented. "How is it blooming already?"

"My grandmother always said that a cool location is the key."

"Your grandmother always gave good advice," Victoria said. "Ava, who is next on the list?"

Ava continued the roll call until eleven ladies and seven cacti were present.

"Now, let's talk about watering our cacti during the winter months. How often do you think it's prudent to water them?" Victoria asked.

"You should definitely let them dry out more between waterings," Alice Fitzpatrick spoke up first. "I always check to be sure that the top three inches of dirt is dry before I add more water." She held up three fingers in front of her heart-shaped face just to ensure that she had been understood.

They talked about watering methods until Ava never wanted to hear the word cactus again. She stifled another yawn, wondering if Floraline was as bored as she was, but her friend truly seemed to be listening to all the older ladies had to say. Floraline had certainly changed. She and her husband Pete, another old school friend, married last year and were expecting their first child. Unlike Estelle, Floraline seemed to be thriving with her pregnancy. Her underdeveloped body was now full, and her cheeks emanated the life within. Pete definitely wouldn't be calling his wife "bean pole" any longer. Looking at her swollen ankles, which were crossed beneath her chair, she wondered if Floraline ever compared her pregnancy to Estelle's.

"Ava, come help me serve the cake," Victoria called, and Ava hopped up, ready for the only good part about her mother's meetings – dessert!

Before long all the women were back in their chairs enjoying slices of lemon pound cake, chocolate pound cake, and butter pound cake.

"You can make a pound cake every bit as delightful as the ones your mother used to make," Delores said before filling her mouth with another bite.

"Thank you, Delores," Victoria replied.

"Ava, have you learned from your mother?" Abigail asked.

"I'm afraid not," Ava answered.

"She's too busy with books and music right now for much else," Victoria said, enjoying her cup of apple cider as much as the cake. It was nice to finally enjoy the product of all her work.

"Speaking of books," Alice joined in. "I heard that Jake Green got to come home this past weekend from medical school to see Rosemary."

All eyes turned to Myrtle, and she almost choked on her cider.

Why does Alice always have to concern herself with my daughter's romantic life? She tried to smile.

"He did," she said when her throat was clear. "They went to hear Ava perform with the Willie Harold Band."

"I think that's lovely." Maris sighed.

"Do you think he'll propose soon this time?" Alice asked.

"I think he needs to focus on his schooling right now," Myrtle said to end the conversation. She had learned not to put too much hope in Rosemary and Jake's relationship. Percy Bledsoe had destroyed any previous ones she had entertained for them. Now, she would just pray.

"You sound just like Francis! I saw her and Dr. Green the other day in town, and she just went on and on and on about how well he was doing in his classes and really giving his medical pursuits his full attention. It's a pity she doesn't think much of Rosemary."

"Rosemary is a fine girl," Victoria interposed. "And Francis Green is blind if she can't see it."

Ava wanted to clap for her mother but thought better of it.

"Floraline, what baby names have you picked out?" Ava asked instead, helping out Myrtle and Rosemary in her own way. By the time the meeting was over, Floraline had a vast assortment of both girl and boy names to consider.

Chapter 5

On Saturdays, Wakefield's Department Store closed at six o'clock instead of five thirty, and as cashier, Rosemary was one of the last to leave. She rattled the heavy door's bells good night and walked out onto Noble Street, clutching the canvas bag which contained the store's night deposit. She would walk it to the First National Bank, leave it in the night drop box, and pick up the deposit slip Monday morning. Even though the bag was locked, she gripped it tight as she wove her way through couples on their way to dinner and families staring at the many window displays lining the sidewalks. The street lamps were just beginning to glow on the cool night, and she shivered, deciding to bring her coat with her to work on Monday. She moved over to make room for a group of teenage boys, and her high heel stuck in a crack in the pavement.

"Good grief," she muttered and moved her foot right and left to dislodge it. Her mother was right; her high heels would be the death of her.

"Need some help," someone asked from behind her, and she froze, feeling as though her whole body might sink through the crevice.

The man touched her elbow, and she jumped away from him, her foot coming out of the shoe.

"Don't touch me," she said as he stooped down and gently jiggled the shoe to remove it.

39

"Is this man bothering you?" An older man who she recognized as a co-worker's husband stopped and asked.

"Oh no, thank you. He's just helping me with my shoe," Rosemary answered, lowering her voice.

The man nodded at her and walked on as Percy retrieved her shoe from the sidewalk.

"Your shoe." He smiled and held it out in his hand.

Their hands met for a moment, and Rosemary recoiled from him again.

"How? Why are you here?" She struggled to put the shoe back on, and he grabbed her elbow again to steady her.

"I can get it!" She shrugged him off. "How can you come near me again?"

She stared up at him, despite herself. It was both awful and wonderful to see him again. Now she knew for sure. He did survive the war which so many others did not. He was no longer in military attire but still had the air of one in charge about him. His black hair was combed back, and he was clean shaven, wearing a suit that was obviously brand new. She had worked in retail long enough to notice all the original fabric creases.

"You have every right to be angry with me, but please hear me out. Just let me walk with you to the bank."

"How do you know where I'm going?"

"You're holding a bag full of money." He laughed, and she started walking, remembering her purpose.

"It's getting dark earlier now. I don't like you walking this to the bank by yourself."

"What I do is my business and no business of yours." She sped up, but he remained by her side.

"Rosemary, she divorced me," he said, and she stopped momentarily. "I'm a free man, and I've been in love with you since the night we first met."

She refused to look at him, knowing his power over her. They were now at the bank. She pulled out a small key from her purse, unlocked the night drop box, and slid in the canvas bag.

"Let me take you to dinner. I'll explain…"

"There is no need to explain anything. You betrayed me and all that I stand for."

"You are so good, Rosemary," he said, and she knew that his eyes were laughing at her even if his mouth wasn't.

"Emogene!" she called out, seeing a girl who worked at S.H. Kress & Co. and who she knew would be taking the same bus home. "Can I walk with you to the bus stop?"

"Sure," Emogene said, visibly admiring the man standing by Rosemary's side.

Rosemary took a step away from Percy, but his hand encircled her wrist and stopped her. For a moment, she thought she felt it tremble.

"I'll let you be, but think about what I said," he whispered in her ear. "I'll be back Monday night to see if your feelings have changed. I love you more than anyone I've ever loved, and I'm sorry I caused you pain. You said before you'd marry me. Do it now."

"Coming Rosemary?" Emogene asked.

Rosemary shrugged off Percy's hand again and left him. She kept her back straight and her step calm as she walked with her friend. She could feel Percy's eyes still on, and she felt as though she might be sick.

"He's handsome," Emogene said, glancing back at Percy.

"If you like that sort," she replied, struggling to breathe.

Rosemary somehow managed to make it off the bus before throwing up in the grass. Luckily, she was the only one getting off at that stop tonight.

I can't go home like this.

Her mother knew her malleable emotions well and would badger her with questions. She pulled out a kerchief from her purse and wiped her face. When she stopped shaking, she decided to walk to Ava's house. Her parents wouldn't worry. They were used to her eating dinner with a friend or seeing a picture show before she came home.

Her whole body felt as if it was breaking, and the way to Ava's house seemed twice as long as normal. She could see lights on in their living room, and she sighed in relief. Thankfully, they were home and not out or next door. Hearing music from the radio, she knocked loudly, and Edwin came to the door.

"Hi Rosemary," he said. "Are you o.k.?"

"I'm fine." She tried to smile but failed. "I just need to see Ava."

"Rosemary!" Ava was now by Edwin's side. "You are not fine. What happened?"

"Can we talk on the porch?"

Ava stepped out and closed the door behind them.

"Sit down," Ava said as tears streamed down her cousin's face and neck, and they sat down side by side on the top step.

"He came to see me," Rosemary finally said, and Ava knew without being told who she was referring to.

"How could he? What did he want?"

"He said his wife divorced him, and he wants me to marry him."

Ava tensed with anger and then fear at what her cousin might do.

"What did you tell him?"

"Nothing, he's coming back..."

"What are you two up to?" Carson yelled out as he passed the house on his way home.

Ava hadn't even seen him coming. She wondered where he had been. Ever since becoming a pastor, he had nothing to do with women.

"Us? Where have you been?" she yelled back.

"Jimmy's back in town for a week," he answered and kept walking. "Goodnight."

"Stop him," Rosemary said.

Ava just looked at her.

"I want to ask him a favor."

"Carson!" Ava called out reluctantly, and he turned back. "Rosemary needs to ask you something."

"This can't be good!" He laughed as he walked up the porch steps. His laughter died as soon as he saw Rosemary's face. Even in the moonlight, the aftermath of her tears could be seen.

"What do you need?" he asked more seriously.

Rosemary told him everything about Percy, and his demeanor gradually changed from one of a taunting cousin to a pastor to a concerned family member. He was used to

43

hearing confessions now from church members but not someone from his own close family.

"I'll do it. I'll talk to him," he said when she was finished, and he put an arm around her trembling shoulders.

Chapter 6

Carson fidgeted with his pocket watch as he waited outside Wakefield's Department Store and scanned the approaching faces for a man he had never met. He had heard his mother and cousin Myrtle venting about the man many times, but he had never actually met Percy. Ava said he favored Clark Gable, and he felt silly looking down the street for someone who looked like a famous actor. He glanced through the store's window and saw Rosemary at her cashier's desk preparing another night deposit. She kept recounting the same tickets, and Carson knew that she was having trouble thinking clearly. The plan was that she would wait and leave after he had got Percy away from the store. He looked back down the sidewalk, and there he was. There was no mistaking him; he did indeed favor the actor.

"Percy!" Carson called out as he stepped toward the unknowing man. "I'm Carson, Rosemary's cousin. She asked me to meet you."

A slow smile spread across Percy's face as he extended his hand toward Carson, and the two men shook hands.

"I'm assuming that by you meeting me here Rosemary doesn't want to talk to me."

"She wants me to talk to you instead, if that's ok," Carson replied, somewhat taken aback by Percy's nonplussed manners. "Want to get a bite to eat?"

"Sure, lead the way," Percy said, and they walked in silence to Vic's Café.

It was quieter in the restaurant than a weekend night would be, and Carson wished it was busier. He didn't want anyone who might know Rosemary overhearing their conversation.

They ordered their dinner, and Carson cleared his throat to begin the difficult discussion, but Percy spoke first.

"Didn't you work with the POWs at Fort McClellan during the war?"

"I did," Carson answered. "Since I was 4-F, I was hired to farm Pelham Range. The officers sent me a crew of prisoners each day to help."

"I always thought it strange to have POWs in the same place you are training men to kill their countrymen."

"I never thought of it like that." Carson frowned, remembering the friends he had made among the German prisoners.

"What were they like? The German and Italian soldiers I met during the war just wanted to blow my brains out."

The waitress came with their food, and as his meatloaf was sat down in front of him, Carson considered Percy's question, realizing how vastly different their war experiences were. No doubt, Percy knew men killed by the German Army.

"They weren't like what I expected," he replied. "Most were decent men just following orders. Good workers. A few were even painters. You should see the murals they painted in the Officer's Club."

"I saw a glimpse of them unfinished once," Percy said, and Carson smiled, remembering his friend Albin and the portrait he painted of his wife.

46

"They certainly fared better than our own men did as prisoners of war," Percy continued.

Carson just swallowed his food, not knowing what else to say. He felt like a traitor and like he always did when he tried to talk to James about the war. Fortunately, James seemed to dodge any war-related conversations.

"Do you still work out at the fort?" Percy asked.

"No, I finished my time there as a POW chaplain. Now, I pastor a church in Heflin, AL and farm with my father."

"A man of God. I hope you made those Germans repent of their sins." Percy smiled. "So, what message does Rosemary have for me?"

Carson laid down his fork, regaining his purpose.

"She wants you to go home and try to work things out with your wife and son."

Percy leaned back in his chair and chuckled.

"Rosemary, Rosemary," he said and leaned forward, lowering his voice. "It's not that simple. I wasn't the only one unfaithful during the war. My ex-wife doesn't love me or want me."

"She may if you give her a reason too." Carson also leaned forward, refusing to back down for his cousin's sake. "What about your son? Shouldn't you make every effort for him?"

"My son doesn't want me around either. When I came back, he treated me like a stranger." Percy's face grew graver rather than angry. "I tried with him, but he seems almost … frightened of me. I don't understand it."

"I'm not a father yet, but love and patience have a way of healing wounds," Carson said, quoting his own father. "My niece is having to learn now who her father is. It takes time."

"I will do what I can for the boy but not his mother. For better or worse, we are finished. She's already engaged to be married again. She obviously never loved me, and I never loved her the way I love Rosemary."

"And if you still love her, you will let her be."

This time it was Percy who said nothing. He breathed deeply and clasped his hands behind his head. The waitress brought their ticket. They paid and walked outside together.

"I could make things right with her this time," Percy said when they were back out on the street.

"She doesn't want that. She still doesn't think it would be right." Carson shifted his weight uncomfortably as Percy's eyes darkened in near desperation.

"Tell her I'll do what she wants." He looked away.

"Thank you." Carson extended his hand. "It was nice to meet you."

"You as well." Percy shook his hand. "I'm going to the fort for a drink. Want to join me? We'll see those murals you talked about."

"I can't tonight."

"Sorry, I forgot you're a man of God. So long, then."

They parted ways, and Carson relaxed. His part was finished. He just hoped Percy would do his.

Rosemary and Ava stood up from where they were sitting on the porch step together when they saw Carson's car approach and come to a stop.

48

"What took so long?" Ava asked when he was out of the car.

"We went to eat dinner."

"We asked you to talk to him not spend the evening with him."

"Ava, don't give him a hard time," Rosemary said. "How did it go?"

"He promised to do what you wanted."

Rosemary sighed and sat back down on the porch step.

"Will he go back to his wife and son then?"

"It doesn't sound like that's an option anymore. Apparently, his wife was also unfaithful and is already about to be married again, and his son doesn't want anything to do with him either."

Rosemary fought back the tears she could feel coming. How could she feel pity for a man who had deceived her?

"It serves him right," Ava said.

"I don't know," Carson replied. "He seemed really hurt by his son."

"I need to go home now." Rosemary stood up.

"Come on. I'll take you," Carson said.

"Thanks and thanks for talking to Percy for me. Ava, thanks for waiting with me."

"You can stay longer if you want," Ava offered. "I can make cookies, and we can play cards."

"Sorry, I'm just exhausted," Rosemary answered. She couldn't wait for the quietness of her room and to be alone for the first time all day.

When they had left, Ava went back inside.

"All over now?" Edwin asked.

"I hope so," she answered and accepted his embrace.

Chapter 7

Victoria had everyone huddled in the living room to read a letter from James, and Ava felt like they were still living during the war except that Edwin was sitting next to her. She poked him in the side just to be sure, and he smiled down at her.

When James had sent home letters from the warfront, it had been a major family event. Each letter had been assurance that he was still alive and might come home. This letter was the first from him since he had taken Ella to live with him a little more than a month ago. Vivie had written several times but not James, and Victoria wanted them all to hear together whatever he had to say.

"Dear family," Victoria cleared her throat and began. "Sorry I haven't written since I last saw you. I know Vivie writes for us often and keeps you updated on Ella. Ella is doing well. She and Vivie are always up to something fun. Work is good, but I have made up my mind to go in a new direction."

At this, Victoria paused and glanced up at her husband, who nodded for her to continue.

"I am going to take advantage of this GI Bill and go to college. I have already been accepted at Georgia Tech and will start studying engineering in January."

"Georgia Tech!" Sheffield leaped up from his chair. "Yes, two in college and one preaching, what more could you ask for!" He slapped Carson on the back.

"That's some fine news," Grandpa Chester agreed from where he sat applying red liniment to his achy elbows.

"You could let me finish the letter before you go jumping up and down," Victoria said.

"Sorry blossom." Sheffield crossed his arms and stood still.

"The government will give us a little living money, but I will still need to work some nights at the airport." Victoria paused again. "Hope everyone is well. We look forward to seeing you all at Christmas. With love, James."

"Christmas?" Victoria gently folded up the letter in her lap. "I was hoping they would come for Thanksgiving."

"That's only another month away, and Vivie has her family too," Sheffield reminded. "Georgia Tech!"

"You sure are excited." Victoria raised an eyebrow at her husband.

"Aren't you?"

"I don't know." She sighed. "I've seen how much Ava has to study and apply herself, and with work, I don't know how much time he will have left over for Ella and Vivie."

Sheffield frowned.

"I'm sure he'll find a way," Carson spoke up for his absent brother.

"A man's gotta provide," Grandpa Chester said. "Let James find his own way."

"I just want Ella to be in it," Victoria replied.

"Vivie will be there when he's not," Ava said, but her mother's firm look told her she had said the wrong thing.

52

"You thinking about doing this GI Bill thing, son?" Grandpa Chester asked Edwin.

"Don't know how good I would be at college, sir," Edwin replied.

"Edwin's doing a good job at the pipe shop," Sheffield said, hoping his enthusiasm over James hadn't belittled his son-in-law.

"He is," Ava agreed and put her hand through Edwin's arm, careful to avoid one of the places she knew he had been burned and scarred.

"Welp," Grandpa Chester said. "This Serviceman's Act or GI Bill as they're calling it sure is helping these boys coming home from the war."

"Mom, it's Bing time." Carson looked at his pocket watch.

"Then turn on the radio!" Victoria sat down and hushed them all with her hands.

Carson turned on the radio, and the Bing Crosby Philco Radio Time Show was announced.

"Give me five minutes more. Only five minutes more. Let me stay, let me stay in your arms," Bing sang to them through the radio, and James's news faded.

Ava smiled to herself as her mother's foot began to bounce up and down to the music. She wasn't the only one who loved the big band.

The next morning, as Ava walked among the red-bricked buildings and landscaped common areas of the Jacksonville State Teachers College, her brother's decision to go to college was on her mind again. She couldn't help but notice all of the young men around her. How many of them were war veterans like James trying to start anew in the world? She now remembered her music professor saying that 500 students that fall were veterans. Looking at the male students, she tried to read it in their faces. A stocky boy in gym clothes was approaching. He waved at her, and she realized that she had been staring. She waved back and quickly walked past him. The steps to Bibb Graves Hall were now at her feet, and she ran up them. Another young man, who seemed older than she was, held the tall, glass door open for her.

"Thank you," she said and hurried down the hall for her first class, imagining where the man had been and what he had seen before he arrived at the college.

Chapter 8

As Rosemary made a neat pile of the tickets she had just reconciled, she heard Mrs. Crockett unlock the front door.

"No need to stand out there in the cold. Come on in. Rosemary is almost ready." Mrs. Crockett held open the door for Jake.

"Thank you, Mrs. Crockett," Jake said, and Rosemary smiled to herself. Jake was the only boy she knew to get special treatment from her manager, who maintained strict rules about young men visiting her unmarried shop girls during working hours. Everyone knew the kind Dr. Green, however, and his like-minded son.

"Busy day?" he asked Mrs. Crockett, taking off his hat and looking around the pristine store.

"Every day is busy at Wakefield's. If not with customers, with preparing the store for customers." Mrs. Crockett placed her hands on her hips and played with the beads around her neck as she surveyed the store for anything else needing her attention before leaving for the night. "All done, Rosemary?"

"Yes, ma'am," Rosemary answered. She was about to put on her coat, but Jake took it from her and helped her with it.

"Thank you," she said, embarrassed somewhat that he would do that in front of her boss.

"You two have a good night." Mrs. Crockett now held the door open for both of them.

"You as well. I'll see you Monday," Rosemary replied.

"She's a nice lady," Jake said once they were out on the street.

"To you!" Rosemary laughed. "Other men often think differently."

Jake held her elbow as they maneuvered the always crowded streets, and as every night after the unexpected visit from Percy, Rosemary's eyes darted from side to side and face to face, making sure that he wasn't about to surprise her again.

"I've missed you," Jake spoke in her ear.

"I would think medical school would keep me out of your thoughts."

He stopped and pulled her to him, the night deposit bag between them.

"Nothing could keep you out of my thoughts." He held her, and she wondered how many people were watching them.

"Your mother wouldn't want to hear that," she said, and he let her go. They were almost at the bank.

"I wish you wouldn't let my mother bother you. She will grow to love you."

"Maybe." Rosemary made her night deposit and put her arm through Jake's. "Now, tell me about your week. How did your exam go?"

He talked about the exam and the new class he was about to begin until they reached the Noble Theater. Rosemary waved when they saw Ava and Edwin waiting for them outside the gazebo-shaped box office.

"I'm not going to lie." Jake lowered his voice. "I wish it were just you and me tonight."

"Next time, then," Rosemary replied, sliding her hand into his.

When Rosemary left the store on the following Monday, no one was waiting for her. Again her eyes scanned the sidewalks for Percy's face. It had been five weeks since Carson talked to him for her, and she still looked for him every night. She wondered if she would ever stop looking for him. Maybe Carson's talk was more persuasive than she imagined it would be.

Later that night, she bent down on her knees on the cold floor, clasped her hands together, and prayed for him. Her mother always told her to take an unsettled mind to God.

"Dear Lord, please bless him. Help him to make things right with his son."

"What ya praying for?" Judith's face popped out from underneath the covers.

"Nothing." Rosemary got up from the floor and lay back down beside her sister. She was thankful she hadn't said his name. Actually, she tried never to say his name. She snuggled up to Judith, who was already breathing hard and asleep again.

Chapter 9

Ava yawned as she watched the bacon sizzle in the frying pan. It was Saturday morning, and she wanted to cook Edwin a breakfast fit for her mother. She was still in her night gown, and it felt good be home with her husband with nowhere to go until that afternoon.

"Good morning," Edwin said, walking into the kitchen in a pair of old work pants.

"Good morning to you," Ava said back and stood on her tip toes to kiss him. His face matched his auburn hair from where he had obviously been scrubbing it with cold water.

"Breakfast will be ready soon. Want your egg runny this morning?

"Are we having biscuits too?"

"Yep, just put them in the oven."

"Then, yes, Mrs. Livingston." He kissed her again and then disappeared into the living room.

Ava heard the radio come on. An advertisement for Bromo Selzer ended, and a male radiobroadcaster began delivering the morning news.

"On this day, December 7, 1946, disaster strikes again in the United States, but this time in Atlanta, GA. Around 3:15 this morning, a fire began at the fifteen-story Winecoff Hotel. It is believed that 119 of the 280 hotel guests have died. Many more are injured."

Ava gripped the counter as Edwin's egg began to burn. She flicked it into the sink and ran to the living room to hear more.

"The bed sheets and ropes hanging from the hotel windows this morning tell the story of those who tried to lower themselves to safety. Many fell to their deaths."

Edwin put his arm around her as they listened to the horrible news together.

"A grief-stricken Atlanta is asking how this could have happened to a hotel advertised to be absolutely fireproof."

The name "Violet Hemmert" and the burning Alabama Hotel leapt into Ava's mind. She felt dizzy as she remembered the awful day when she and Rosemary witnessed the destruction of the once grand hotel in Anniston. Violet had been a young wife visiting her husband at Fort McClellan. The burning was so close in time to Estelle's death that the two events always merged in her mind as one great tragedy, and tears began to make their way down her cheeks and moisten her gown.

"We'll pray for them," Edwin said, pulling her to him, and he held her as the news story ended and talk of the 5th Anniversary of Pearl Harbor Remembrance ceremonies began.

"The biscuits!" Ava said and hurried back in the kitchen. She took them out of the oven and sighed in relief when she saw that they were only slightly browner than she would have liked.

A little butter will take care of that, she thought.

She started over on their eggs, and soon they sat down to eat their leisurely breakfast.

"I can't imagine what it must be like to be awoken in the middle of the night by a fire," Ava said, watching the yellow center of her egg ooze out onto her plate and surround her biscuit.

"It's frightening," Edwin replied.

Ava looked up, not sure which experience he was referring to.

"Waking up to bombs I imagine would be very similar," he explained as he sopped up his egg with his biscuit.

"Did that happen often?" She was careful not to appear too eager. He told her very little about his time in the war, saying that it had caused enough trouble and shouldn't be allowed to cause anymore. She failed to understand how talking about it could do more damage.

"More often than any of us would have liked."

"What was it like?"

"Terrifying. At first, you are startled and have to remember where you are and what your situation is. Then, something inside of you takes over and you do whatever it takes to stay alive. It's something you never forget. I'm sure the survivors of this fire will have a hard time of it."

Ava put a hand over Edwin's. *Are you still having a hard time of it?* She wanted to ask out loud but didn't.

"What time do we leave?" he asked. She withdrew her hand and let him eat his bacon.

"Willie said the bus leaves at 3:00."

At three o'clock, Ava and Edwin were on their way to the Redstone Arsenal in Huntsville, AL for a Pearl Harbor Remembrance Day performance with the Willie Harold Band. The few times before when Ava had rode the bus with the band it had been loud with singing and shouting across aisles. Today, it was almost quiet as everyone conversed in hushed tones. This performance was of a more somber nature, and everyone had their thoughts in Atlanta.

They arrived at the arsenal, and Edwin helped unload instruments and equipment.

"My sister worked here for two years during the war," a saxophone player named Clifford told them as they set up chairs.

"Is that so?" Edwin said.

"She was a tool-crib operator. Believe it or not, this whole place used to be covered with women or 'soldiers of production' like they were called."

"None of them are here anymore?" Ava asked, thinking of Vivie.

"Nope. Got rid of them all last October after the war was over. Can you believe they paid Lucille five dollars a day? I think she misses the pay more than she does the work!"

Ava hid a smile, remembering that this was a paid performance. She, along with every band member, was getting paid today, and it felt good. She couldn't help but feel sorry, though, for all the women who no longer had work after the war.

"Ok band, let's warm up!" Willie Harold's voice rose over the chatter, and soon everyone and everything was in place.

After a short warm-up, it was already time to perform. The room was suddenly full of arsenal personnel and their guests.

"History in every century records an act that lives forevermore. We'll recall, as in to line we fall, the thing that happened on Hawaii's shore," Ava sang Don Reid's and

Sammy Kaye's tribute to those who fell at Pearl Harbor. "Let's remember Pearl Harbor as we go to meet the foe."

A week later, the Winecoff Hotel blazed again in Ava's heart through a letter from Vivie. It was the first one Vivie had written to her personally, and she ripped it open, honored that her sister-in-law would write to her alone. It reminded her of the letters Estelle used to write to her from Texas when James was in basic training. Apprehension now steadied her hand. *Is something wrong? Is that why she is writing to me?*

Hello Ava,

What a sad week! I am sure you heard about the Winecoff. A man James and I had just met at the airport passed away in the fire. His name was Harold Irvin. He was a Navy pilot during the war and was here with his brother to find a job as a commercial pilot. Eastern Airlines had already offered him a job. He seemed so nice. He was only 23. How sad to survive the war and then end up in the worst hotel fire our country has seen. His brother survived.

Now, to happier things. Ella is doing well. I think she is going to take after you. She sings all the time. I encourage her to sing as loud and as much as she wants!

Your mother wrote to me that your grandparents from Birmingham are visiting for Christmas. Please tell me all about them. James says that even your mother is scared of your Grandma Lavenia. Do tell me all about her and anything that would help me make a good impression.

Can't wait to see you for the holidays!

With much love,

Vivie

So, Grandma is why she wrote to me, Ava thought and laughed. *It's going to be an unforgettable Christmas!*

Chapter 10

The Stilwell house was spotless and festively dressed with holly and crocheted stockings when Jack and Lavenia Stilwell arrived from Birmingham on Christmas Eve. It was only the second time that Ava could ever remember them visiting. They saw them once a year but always in Birmingham, where her grandfather's prosperous grocery business was and where her grandmother was known by all.

Ava looked at her mother who was trying to sit calmly next to her grandmother and bit her lip to suppress a smile. Victoria had worked non-stop over the past two weeks and could not keep her hands and feet still, afraid that there was still something left undone, something in their modest house not up to her mother-in-law's standards.

"You keep a fine house," Lavenia said and sipped her cup of hot tea, which Victoria had ready the minute she walked through the door.

"Thank you," Victoria replied, her whole body exhaling.

"Keeping up with the war news, son?" Jack Stilwell asked Sheffield from his place by the fire.

"But the war is over," Ava said.

"Yes, but not officially. I'm assuming you're talking about the announcement Truman is supposed to make after

Christmas," Sheffield answered first his daughter and then his father.

"We need an official end to this bad business." Jack shook his head. "Had two boys from the war return to the grocery store recently. It's time for them to look forward and not back anymore. You agree?" He looked over at Edwin.

"Yes, sir," Edwin replied.

"Official statement or not," Grandpa Chester spoke up. "Those Nazis and Japs have been beat, and that's the end of the story."

"Mr. Stilwell, wouldn't you like a chair now?" Victoria offered, hoping her father wouldn't offer any more of his opinions.

"Oh, let him stand." Lavenia waved her hand dismissively. "He prefers it that way."

"Been sitting in that car far too long already," Jack said.

"When are James and Ella and this new wife expected to be here?" Lavenia asked.

"The way James drives, any minute," Carson said.

"He better not be driving too fast with that baby in the car!"

"He'll be careful," Sheffield said.

"So, tell me about this Miss Vivie."

"Sweet girl from Marietta, GA," Sheffield told his mother. "I'm sure you will like her."

"I haven't met many from Georgia that I took a strong liking to. They always think they are better than us Alabamians."

Ava laughed, and Victoria gave her a stern look.

"Well, your grandson is making Georgia his home now, so you better change your opinion of them," Jack said.

"What do you think of her?" Lavenia asked her daughter-in-law.

"She's making an excellent mother for Ella," Victoria answered truthfully. "She's spirited and has a very unusual laugh."

"Victoria!" Sheffield said.

"There's nothing wrong in saying that. Many people have unusual laughs."

Ava and Carson both had pain in their sides from trying not to laugh themselves.

"How is it unusual?" Lavenia ignored her son.

"Just very loud and frequent."

"I would rather have that than a constant frowner," Sheffield said.

Just then, a car was heard outside, and Victoria instantly forgot about her in-laws and everything else. Her granddaughter was back, and she was out the door and holding Ella before anyone else had even made it on the porch.

Ava sat inside with her grandmother. To Lavenia Stilwell, patience was a southern lady's virtue, and she waited with tea cup in hand for them all to come to her.

"You didn't tell me anything about Miss Vivie," she said to Ava.

"I'm very thankful that James and Ella have her," Ava replied, and the front door opened.

"Ava! Mrs. Stilwell!" Vivie came running in.

She hugged Ava first and then almost spilled Lavenia's tea, hugging her as well.

"Goodness gracious," Lavenia said. "What excitement!"

"I am very excited to meet you." Vivie laughed, and Lavenia jumped with the noise.

"How was your trip?" Ava asked as her grandmother tried to regain her composure. Any composure was short lived, however, now they both noticed Vivie's outfit. She wore a thin, black blouse and long, beige slacks. The slacks were tight about her waist with a wide band and tiny leather belt but flowed out at her hips and fell loosely about her legs.

"You're both looking at my slacks. Do you like them?" Vivie asked and turned for them to get a better look.

Ava didn't know how to answer. How could Vivie wear pants in front of her grandmother, the woman who dressed as if every day was Sunday. She had specifically written to her about how they all dress in their best for her grandmother.

"I know Katherine Hepburn and Ginger Rogers are trying to get women to dress like men, but I don't think much of it," Lavenia said. "You are a pretty thing, though."

"Thank you, Mrs. Stilwell." Vivie smiled. "If you ever wore pants, you would change your mind. I didn't think I would like them either until I had to wear them at the Bell Bomber plant."

"I will never be working in a factory, so I don't think I'll be trying them," Lavenia said and sipped her now cold tea.

The front door opened again, and Jack, Sheffield, Victoria, and Ella entered with James, Carson, and Edwin following behind with armfuls of luggage.

"I still don't know why girls, even little girls, require so much," James said.

"There's my great grandbaby!" Lavenia stood up, and Victoria presented Ella to her. Vivie might not be dressed up to Lavenia's liking but her great granddaughter was. She wore a red and green plaid dress with a white eyelet collar. She hugged the little girl and then looked around for James. "Don't I get a hug?"

James hugged his grandmother.

"Did you met Vivie?" he asked and put an arm around his wife.

"She seems lovely," Lavenia said, glancing down at Vivie's slacks again.

The night was full of eating ham, deviled eggs, and red velvet cake and singing Christmas carols. Even though Lavenia had never been one to sing in public, she loved listening to her son and his family. Jack tried to join them but always managed to be in a different key or part of the song than the rest of the group.

"Jack, why don't you just listen?" Lavenia tugged on her husband's shirt sleeve and laughed.

"You can sing with me." Vivie laughed too. "I don't fit in with this family musically either!"

"Nonsense, it takes all kinds of voices to make a heavenly choir," Sheffield said. "Mother, you should sing too."

"Listening to all of you is enough for me."

"Why don't you all let Ella sing for you now?" Vivie suggested.

"Do you have a special Christmas song for us?" Sheffield bent down and picked up his granddaughter.

Ella nodded, and they all grew quiet waiting for her voice.

"Jingle bells, jingle bells, jingle all the way," she sang quietly at first, but all of their smiling faces encouraged her to sing louder. "Jingle bells, jingle bells, jingle all the way."

"That was beautiful!" Victoria clapped.

"Like an angel," Grandpa Chester agreed.

"We're working on the rest of the words," Vivie said.

"James, have you been singing and playing the banjo for her?" Lavenia asked.

"Not much," James replied. "That performance is all Vivie."

Ava saw her mother look at Vivie who shook her head slightly in return.

"Well, looks like we may have two accomplished songstresses in the family one day," Lavenia said. "Ava, have you performed with the band recently?"

"We just performed in Huntsville."

"I think it's high time you come back to Birmingham."

"Hopefully, one day."

"College going well? Studying hard?" Jack asked.

"I try to," Ava said.

"That reminds me," Sheffield interrupted. "We have another member of the family about to enter college."

"Which one?" Lavenia looked from James to Carson to Vivie and her pants.

"James will be attending Georgia Tech in the new year!"

"Well, I'll be!" Jack patted his grandson on the back. "That's some fine news."

"Thank you," James said.

"We wanted to tell you in person." Sheffield grinned. Despite his wife's reservations, he couldn't help but revel in the news he had been waiting to tell.

They talked until it was late and everyone was ready for bed. Ava and Edwin left but not before promising to come back early the next morning for Christmas breakfast.

"Ava, wake up!" Edwin shook Ava's shoulder and then kissed her cheek.

She swatted at his face and then gradually opened her eyes to find him smiling over her with a present in hand.

"What time is it?" She yawned.

"Time for you to get up. I can't wait to give this to you any longer."

"Is the sun even up?"

"About to be."

Ava could see a spark of light starting to grow through the curtains. She rubbed her eyes and noticed again what he had in his hands.

"Here," he said, holding the rectangular package out.

She sat up and took it from him. It was wrapped in candy-cane striped paper, and she could tell by the uneven corners that he had wrapped it himself. She held it up to her ear and shook it. A small thud was heard as whatever it was moved from side to side.

"A hat pin?"

"Maybe."

She tore off the paper to find an old shoebox.

"Men's shoes! Just what I needed." They laughed, and she opened the box to find a smaller box inside.

"Clever," she said.

70

"I couldn't make it easy for you."

She lifted the lid of the box and found a ring sitting in its center. It had a silver band with two curved rows of emeralds and a row of diamonds in between.

"Edwin!"

"Do you like it? The jeweler said that every woman needs a birthstone ring."

"I love it, but you shouldn't have spent so much money on me. I thought we were saving for a car."

"We are, but that doesn't mean I can't buy my wife something nice for Christmas."

He took the ring out of the box and slid it onto her right ring finger.

"If it's too loose, the jeweler said we could bring it back to be resized."

"It's perfect!" She held her hand out and gazed down at it.

"It is," he agreed, looking at her face instead of the ring.

"Wait!" She jumped off the bed and reached under it. "This is for you," she said, resurfacing with a package wrapped in crisp red paper and a white bow. All of the corners held tight to what was underneath as Mrs. Crockett had instructed her many times during her employment at Wakefield's.

She held it out to him but withdrew it when he reached for it.

"Remember, I didn't know we could spend so much on each other."

"Just give it to me." He laughed.

She gave the package to him, and he unwrapped it to find a brown, leather case. Inside was a tin of talc, a Gillette Gold razor, three brushes, a nail clipper, and a comb.

"You said you needed a new razor," she explained.

"I did. It's nice."

"You should try it out before we go see grandma again this morning."

"Are you saying my face is too scruffy for your grandma?" He laughed.

"Maybe, a little but not for me." She ran her fingers over his face and then kissed him.

"I'll shave but you have to show everybody your new ring."

Ava lay back on the bed and held up her hand to the stream of sunlight now coming through the slight part in their curtains. Edwin lay down next to her.

"It reminds me of a butterfly," she said.

"It kind of does." He pulled her hand down and held it. "Merry Christmas."

"Merry Christmas," she said back. It was their second Christmas together, and it was as perfect as the ring.

When they made it back for breakfast, they found Victoria waiting for them on the porch with a dishpan in hand.

"What took you two so long? Everyone is almost finished eating. I hope your gravy isn't cold."

"Merry Christmas, Mom," Ava said, putting out her hand.

"Isn't that pretty." Victoria sat down the pan and admired Ava's ring. "Edwin, you know how to spoil my daughter."

72

"I try," Edwin said.

"Before you go showing it off, Ava, I'm going to tell you what I already told Carson this morning." Victoria glanced back at the door and lowered her voice. "No joking around today. Your grandma's nerves have had enough of Vivie's laugh."

"Mom!" Ava sighed. "It's Christmas. Everyone should be allowed to laugh."

"Just don't give her any more incentive."

"I'll do my best."

"Thank you." Victoria picked back up the dishpan and motioned for them to go on inside. "At least she's wearing a dress today."

"I liked the pants," Ava said as Edwin opened the door and held it for them.

"Ava!"

Ava didn't have to respond. Her grandfather had seen them and was calling them to the table.

Chapter 11

Watermelon – that was all Ava could think of as she watched Hazel Wheeler, her music teacher, write out a portion of their song on the chalkboard. Her Grandpa Chester's watermelons were always red and juicy in the inside even if their outside was rather small. It would be some months before this year's crop was ready, but she could already taste them.

"Let's sing this part again," Mrs. Wheeler said and sat down behind her piano. "It's a quick piece and easy to forget proper annunciation. Pronounce every beginning and ending consonant. Here are the words. Even though you know them, read them as you sing."

"Oh, when the drums begin to bang," Ava sang out with all the other girls. "Oh, when the drums begin to bang. Lord, I want to be in that number, when the saints go marching in."

She worked on her annunciation as she thought of lightly salting a large wedge of watermelon.

What's wrong with me? It's not like I didn't eat breakfast or lunch or peanuts in between.

"That's all we have time for today." Mrs. Wheeler stood up from behind her piano and ended their class.

"Want to get an ice cream?" Ava asked her friend Rebekah sitting next to her.

"It's a cold day for ice cream, but why not!"

They put on their coats and gathered up their books. The Westend Drug Store was on the Jacksonville Square, so they would have a bit of a walk in the January air.

"Did you hear my stomach growling in class?" Ava asked.

"No," Rebekah replied. "Too busy annunciating."

"Good. I don't know why I'm so hungry today."

"My aunt Millie is pregnant, and my mom says she must be having triplets by the way she's eating."

Ava stopped, a look of alarm overcoming her face.

"You're not expecting are you?" Rebekah stopped too.

"Of course not," Ava said and walked a little faster. *I can't be pregnant*, she told herself. *Of course, it's possible but not now.*

"Ava, did you hear me?" Rebekah asked. "What kind of ice cream are you getting?"

"Have you ever heard of watermelon ice cream?"

"That does not sound good!"

"Why not? Everyone eats strawberry ice cream."

They made it to the drugstore, and Ava had one scoop of vanilla and one scoop of chocolate. She wasn't as hungry anymore, but she couldn't get Rebekah's Aunt Millie off her mind.

What if I am pregnant? The same question kept repeating itself once Rebekah was gone and she was on her way home. *Floraline!*

Ava found her friend Floraline outside hanging up laundry. Even though it was cold, she wore no coat, and the sleeves of her dress were pushed up to her elbows. Her cheeks were red, and she panted each time she had to bend over for a garment. She was certainly bigger than the last time Ava had seen her.

Her delivery can't be far off. Did Mom say February or March?

"Let me hand those to you," Ava said, reaching into her basket.

"Ava! What a good surprise!" Floraline took a pair of Pete's overalls from her and began to hang them on the line.

"I just stopped by to check on you."

"I'll be better next month when this baby is born!"

So, it is February.

"I'm so tired all the time, and I've started getting nose bleeds like those ones Aggie used to have in grammar school," Floraline told her.

"Sounds terrible," Ava said and handed her the last shirt in the basket.

"It will all be worth it."

"I hope... I'm sure it will be."

"Mind carrying that basket in the house for me?"

"Not at all." Ava picked up the basket and followed behind.

Floraline and Pete lived in a converted sharecropper's house on the Gunters' property. It was an old house, but Pete's constant work on it made it comfortable. Ava still didn't know how he did it all with his war injury. Everyone pitied him when he first came home from the war, but, somehow, he managed do the work of two men. She always wondered if the injury actually made him a greater man than he would have been otherwise.

"You can just sit the clothes down anywhere," Floraline said once they were in the house. She sat down on the couch and propped her feet up on a box on the floor. "Ava, you don't mind seeing my legs do you?"

"No, I've seen them before." Ava smiled.

Floraline pulled her dress up to her thighs and fanned herself with a LIFE magazine.

"I'm just so hot all the time."

"At least it's January and not July." Ava sat down in the rocking chair across from her. The cover of the magazine Floraline kept flapping in front of her pictured a woman modeling beach resort fashion, and Ava thought of how out of place it seemed in her friend's house at the moment.

"You been in class today?" Floraline asked.

"Yes, Christmas break is over."

"College must be a lot more exciting than doing house chores all day with a body this big."

"You haven't felt bad your whole time have you?" Ava asked, trying to figure out how to ask the question she wanted answered most.

"No, but now it's just so hard to do anything."

"I'm glad the beginning was easy for you."

"It was. Besides my chest aching a little, I felt great."

"Why hello, Siren!" Pete called out as he opened the front door. It was the nickname he had called her since they were in school together. Ava sighed. Her conversation with Floraline was over.

"Hi Pete."

"Ava came to check on me," Floraline said without getting up.

"We should have a baby any day now!" Pete hobbled in, his disjointed leg trailing his good one. Ava always tried to focus her eyes on his face and not his leg.

"It will be a few more weeks," Floraline corrected.

"You'll have to send word as soon as the baby is here," Ava said.

"I'll run over and tell you myself." Pete laughed. Ava smiled, but she didn't like joking about his injury.

"Hey, tell your father to come see me," Pete said now. "The government is paying me as a veteran to take this farming class. I know far more on the matter than the teacher, but it is giving me ideas. Thinking about experimenting with soybean. Pa and Edgar aren't keen on it, but it may just be the future of farming for us."

"Can you believe they are paying him for that?" Floraline asked.

"I'll take anything Uncle Sam wants to give me." Pete laughed, and this time, Ava did too. The war had done many sad things, but it had also done some funny things.

Chapter 12

Rosemary flipped down the wintery garden scene and sat the January page of the Brown's Funeral Home courtesy calendar down next to the December calendar page that Ava had already placed on the table.

"How can you not remember when your last cycle was?"

"I don't like to think about it." Ava placed her pen on January 14, 1947, the day's date, and began to travel back with it through the calendar.

"Why don't you place a tiny dot on the day you start each month like I do so you will know when it is likely to occur again?"

"Why do you want to anticipate the awful?" Ava asked back, and Rosemary sighed.

"What can you remember then about your last one?"

"Oh!" Ava said. "I remember that I was hoping it would be over before the concert in Huntsville. I didn't want to feel bad performing."

"When was the concert?"

Ava looked now at the December calendar.

"It was Pearl Harbor Remembrance Day. So, December 7."

"Then that would be over six weeks ago. You probably are expecting."

Ava sat looking at the calendars, tears beginning to surface. *Not now,* she thought as she felt an imagined or real pain in her chest just like the ones Floraline had described.

Rosemary put a conciliatory hand on her shoulder.

"Aren't you excited to have a baby?"

"I know I should be." She could no longer hold back the tears. They fell down her cheeks and dotted the calendars.

"Why aren't you?" Rosemary grabbed the kitchen towel on the stove and handed it to her.

"You were there." Ava blotted her eyes and face with the towel. "You remember all Estelle suffered and what happened that horrible night."

"That doesn't happen most of the time. Your mom had you and Carson and James with no troubles. My mom had me and Judith. Floraline hasn't been sick like Estelle."

"I'm also still in college. I want to finish. I can't do that with a baby, and what about the band?"

"Why would the band care if you have a baby? You can sing just as good with or without one." Rosemary didn't mention college. That part probably would be over for her cousin. She had never heard of a woman with a baby in college. "I'm sure Edwin and your mom will help look after it during your performances."

"I can't tell them yet," Ava said, stifling her tears. "I can't tell until I learn to be happy about this first."

"I'll help you. We can look at baby clothes at the store or something," Rosemary offered, and Ava burst out in tears again.

Bibb Graves Hall was on fire! Ava stumbled back and then ran away from it with the other students.

"Hurry!" Rebekah called back to her.

Ava tried to run faster, but her legs didn't want to move. The fire was closer. Floraline ran past her, her large abdomen leading the way. Ava looked back and screamed as the flames seemed to be reaching toward her. Suddenly, she was no longer running. She was home and rushing in the front door to find Edwin. Someone else was sitting in James's arm chair. It was Estelle.

"You made it!" Estelle smiled up at her. She was in her night gown and cradling something in her arms. At first, Ava thought it was a kitten but then realized it was a baby.

"Ava! Ava!" Edwin's voice called to her, and she woke up trembling. "What were you dreaming about? You've been trying to run off the bed."

"The college was on fire." She sat up. "I couldn't run fast enough."

"You're here with me, Songbird. You're safe." He pulled her down onto his chest and put his arms around her. She could hear his heart beating. "I'm sure it's that Winecoff Fire making you have bad dreams. Try to think about something happier."

"I will," she said, but it was no longer the fire consuming her mind. It was Estelle in the ivory nightgown she died in, holding on to that baby.

Edwin went back to sleep, and Ava lay listening to his heart beat until she too finally fell asleep.

Chapter 13

Rosemary held the tiny shoes in her hands. They were simple and white but beautiful.

It's their size that makes them so precious, she thought. She sat them down on the counter, filled out a ticket, and paid for them.

"Baby shower present?" Mrs. Crocket asked in passing.

"For a friend," Rosemary replied.

"Excellent gift choice. Perfect for a baby boy or baby girl."

Mrs. Crockett was on the other side of the store now, and Rosemary carefully wrapped the shoes in tissue paper. If these shoes couldn't make Ava happy about becoming a mother, she didn't know what would. It had been just over two weeks since Ava discovered she was pregnant, and Rosemary still couldn't get her to tell Edwin or her parents. She placed the shoes in her purse and got her coat. Jake was home and about to meet her. It would be just the two of them tonight. He wanted a "nice dinner and a long walk around Oxford Lake." She feared he wanted to discuss their future again. The baby shoes did make her a little more inclined on the subject. Regardless, she was resolute. She would honor his mother in this. He must finish medical school and be sure of himself and her before anything further between them could be decided. She picked up the night deposit bag and walked to the door.

"Goodnight," she called out to Mrs. Crockett.

"Goodnight, dear. See you Monday."

Rosemary closed the door behind her, turned, and met Percy. She dropped the bag and her purse with the baby shoes.

"Percy!" she gasped, both hands gripping her chest.

"Hi Rosemary." He stepped and then stumbled toward her. Something was wrong with him. He was unshaven, and his shirt was undone. "Guess you never expected to see me again. Thought your cousin had gotten rid of me."

Before she could respond, Jake was there. He punched Percy in the face, and Percy fell backward onto the sidewalk. Rosemary screamed and ran to where he lay.

"Are you ok?" She cupped Percy's head in her hands.

He groaned, and she looked up at Jake. He was wearing his navy suit with a new cream handkerchief and holding a small bouquet of red and white roses.

"How could you?" she asked, and their eyes met. In that moment, she couldn't hide or deny that she had and still loved the man lying beside her whether he deserved it or not.

"I see," Jake spoke, and the bouquet of roses dropped from his hand and scattered on the ground around her.

They then realized that people were stopped and watching.

"Goodbye, Rosemary," he said and walked away.

Rosemary's head dropped onto Percy's chest, and she cried for both the man in her lap and the man who had just left her.

"Rosemary, don't cry." Percy gripped her hand. "I'll make everything right."

Ava lay in bed wishing the sun would come up. She was tired of trying to sleep. More fiery bad dreams and worries had disrupted her rest. Edwin breathed deeply beside her, unconcerned for the baby he knew nothing about. A soft tap on the front door silenced her thoughts.

Who's here so early? Mom? Dad?

She tiptoed to the door and turned on the porch light. It was her father.

"What's wrong?" she asked, stepping out on the porch.

"Rosemary's left."

Ava felt all the blood drain from her face. She didn't have to ask who her cousin left with.

"Did you know she was leaving?"

"No, I had no idea."

Sheffield began to pace and run his fingers through his hair.

"We don't know what to do," he said more to himself than to her. "Come to the house. Your mother and Myrtle want to talk to you too."

"Of course." Ava stepped back in the door and grabbed her coat. She wouldn't bother changing out of her nightgown. She started to leave and remembered Edwin. She walked back to the bedroom, shook him awake, and told him she had to go to her parents for a little while.

"Why?" he asked, realizing how early it was.

"I'll tell you when I get back."

Ava left without letting him ask any more questions. Her father was still pacing the porch when she joined him.

"Did you know this Percy was back again?"

"No," Ava replied. Her first emotion was heartbreak. Now, it was betrayal. She thought Rosemary told her everything.

"Carson told us about Percy coming back in October and how Rosemary asked him to persuade him not to come back again."

"She did, and he told Carson he would do as Rosemary wished," Ava said and realized she hadn't believed him herself. The man had proven to be a selfish liar. "When did she leave with him?"

"Last night after she came home from work. Myrtle said she looked unwell, but Rosemary insisted she had eaten something that didn't agree with her. They thought she went to bed, but instead, she packed a small bag, wrote them a letter, and snuck out after they were all asleep. Judith woke them up early this morning saying she couldn't find her sister."

The feeling of betrayal Ava felt now turned back to heartbreak, and she swallowed hard to keep from crying.

"Where did they go?"

"We don't know for sure. The letter said they were getting married and that he had job prospects up north."

All the blood drained from Ava's face again. She felt like her cousin had been taken from them. The heartbreak changed to anger at the man she wished they had never met.

They were now inside the house. Judith was in Victoria's lap crying, and Myrtle was standing behind them sobbing into a tissue. Jude had a hand on his wife's shoulder but was turned away from them. Carson sat at the table with his head in his hands, and Ava couldn't tell if he was sleeping or praying. Grandpa Chester was still in his room, probably asleep and oblivious to it all. He had done his share of worrying over children in life.

"She didn't know Percy was back again or that Rosemary was leaving," Sheffield said.

"She never mentioned anything at all to you about this man trying to contact her again?" Victoria asked her daughter. Her tone was angry, and Ava felt as though she were being accused of something.

"No! She thought after Carson spoke to him that he wouldn't come back."

"I think I'll go to the police," Jude turned and spoke, his one good eye hard and glistening while his glass eye, the one he got after a hunting accident, looked lazily ahead.

"I don't know if it will do any good, but we can try," Sheffield said. "I'm afraid they will just say that she's an adult and can marry as she likes."

"Go," Myrtle said between sobs. "Try anything to get her back."

Carson followed his dad and Jude out the door. Myrtle cried louder, and Ava went to her. She wasn't used to consoling like her mother, but she would try. She put her arms around Myrtle and now cried herself. They stayed that way for some time until Victoria sat Judith on her own two feet and stood up.

"We can sit here and cry all morning or we can actually do something to help." Victoria walked over to the couch, got down on her knees, and clasped her hands. Judith knelt down beside her older cousin as close as she could get. Ava let go of Myrtle, and they too knelt down.

"Lord," Victoria began. "We ask you to help Rosemary. If it is your will, we pray that she will leave this man and come home to us. If she does not, we ask you to bless her. We ask you to give her a happy marriage and to take care of her wherever she may go. Lord, thank you for Rosemary, who has been like another daughter to me. We commit her to you."

They now knelt in silence and then in tears again until the men returned. Their dejected faces answered their questions before any words were spoken.

"She's not a child anymore. The police can do nothing," Sheffield said.

Chapter 14

Ava watched from her kitchen window as Pete shuffled and skipped toward their house. He was true to his word. It did appear that he was trying to run with his news, bad leg or not! She hurried out the door and met him in front of the house, wanting to save him some trouble.

"Ava, the baby's here!" Pete shouted with a big, contagious grin across his face.

"Congratulations!" Ava called back, smiling herself. It felt good to smile. She felt as though she hadn't smiled in days. "Boy or girl?"

"Another Gunter boy!"

"And his name?"

"Eugene, after an army buddy of mine who wasn't as lucky."

"I like it. How's Floraline?" Ava asked.

"Recuperating. She says she feels as though she's been torn in two," he replied, and Ava winced.

"I'll come by and see her tomorrow if you think she would like that."

"She would love it. She's so happy! She wants everyone to see the baby!"

"Then, tell her I'll come."

"Gotta run find Carson!"

Ava laughed as she watched his right leg skip and his left leg shuffle behind toward her parents' house now.

Will Edwin be that happy? She ran her fingers across her abdomen and walked back inside. She would make cookies for when she visited Floraline the next day.

The peanut butter cookies were packed and ready to be taken to the Gunters' house. Ava carried them out the door and found a box addressed to her along with the mail. The mailman must have come after she fell asleep reading about Beethoven's musical childhood. The handwriting was a tight, loopy cursive, and she knew at once who it was from. *Rosemary!*

She took the cookies back inside the house and pried open the box with her fingernails. There was a note and something else. *What is it?* She unwrapped the item carefully. *Baby shoes?* They were small enough to hold in one hand, and she stared down at them as tears clouded their image. She sat the shoes down, blinked back the tears she was tired of, and picked up the note.

Dear Ava,

I am sorry to have left without talking to you first. Last Friday night is all a jumbled memory. I was meeting Jake, and then Percy showed up. It wasn't good. I can't explain it. I never dreamed this would happen. Percy needs me, and, somehow, I find I still love him. We are married. We got married in a courthouse in Frankfort, Kentucky. Please try to be happy for me. I miss you and Mom and Dad and Judith all terribly, but I am happy to be his wife and to help him find his way. We are headed to Detroit. Percy has a job opening there. He wants to start over and make a new life for us.

I bought these shoes for you the day I left. I hope they will help you find peace about having a baby. Think about the sweet feet that will be filling them and don't worry. You must tell Edwin and your parents. They will help you have courage. I will also be praying blessings on you every day.

Please tell Mom and Dad that I am happy and not to worry about me. I know they are hurt and angry. I have also written to Mrs. Crockett, but if you see her, please tell her thanks for everything from me. I will write again when we have a place to live and an address to send you.

Love,
Rosemary

Ava refolded the note and picked back up the baby shoes. The leather was smooth and soft.

"Can a real person with feelings, wants, and needs start life this small?" she whispered to the empty house.

She wrapped the shoes back in the tissue paper and took them and Rosemary's note to her bedroom. She needed to hide them for the moment. Her eyes scanned the room and then rested on the hope chest her Grandpa Chester had made for them last Christmas. Inside were extra blankets, something that Edwin never needed. He was always hot, and she was always cold. She stuffed the shoes and note between the double folds of the bottom quilt.

"Now to the Gunters," she told herself. She would have to hurry if she was going to make it home before Edwin. Cookies back in hand, she rushed out the door with Rosemary's note replaying in her mind.

Lord, grant me peace about this baby and bless Rosemary, she prayed.

Chapter 15

Victoria arranged alternating slices of banana nut and zucchini bread on a plate while Ava stirred sugar in the tea and Myrtle set out glass cups.

"I just don't think I should have come today," Myrtle said for the tenth time as two of the cups clinked together in her hands.

"Why don't you sit down and collect yourself." Victoria took the cups out of her hands and to the safety of the table before pulling out a chair for her. "Of course, you should have come! You can't run from the whole community forever."

"I just don't know if I can talk about Rosemary leaving yet without making a scene." Myrtle's voice cracked, and Victoria steadied her emotions with her gaze.

"All you have to do is tell them the truth. Nothing more." Victoria now glanced up at Ava, and Ava took over the cups.

"When you are asked, and I'm sure that nosy Alice will," Victoria continued, "just say that Rosemary married a lieutenant she met during the war who was stationed at Fort McClellan."

"What if they want to know where she is?"

"She's in Michigan where he's getting a job at an automobile plant."

"Ok." Myrtle sighed "I'll try."

"There'll be no trying Myrtle Bonds, just doing. I don't want to see what has happened get you down any longer." Victoria set the plate of bread down with a thud in the center of the table, and Myrtle jumped and then nodded.

Ava looked up at her mother's taut face and busy hands, which were now lifting a chair to be taken into the living room. Her mother despised self-defeat, and she wouldn't allow it in those she loved.

"Ava, grab some chairs. Garden club members should be here any second."

Ava did as she was told, giving her older cousin the most reassuring smile she could manage on the way out.

The chairs were all in a circle and filling fast. Ava sat with the roster ready to call roll when asked. She felt sorry for Myrtle, who was sitting across from her giggling at every small comment, an undisguised look of panic across her face as her green eyes darted from person to person to see who was going to ask the question first. Ava thought her hair had more grey sprinkles, and she was beginning to believe her mother's saying that worry aged a person more than time.

"That baby is all fat and wrinkles!" Delores Waters said of Floraline's baby, and Ava missed her friend who was at home with the fat baby.

"That's the best kind of baby," Alice Fitzpatrick replied. "That means the milk is coming as it should."

Ava cringed, and the front door opened again. This time it was Ingrid Carson, her often sick and absent aunt. There was an open chair next to Myrtle, and Ingrid lumbered toward it. Ava was always fearful that their chairs wouldn't support her overweight aunt.

"Hello ladies," Ingrid greeted. "Hello Myrtle, what's this I hear about Rosemary getting married? Shouldn't her family know about that sort of thing?"

Just like that, the room was silent, all other conversations forgotten mid-sentence.

Myrtle looked around the room and opened her mouth but nothing came out. Ava noticed her mother start to speak but then think better of it.

"Is she married or not?" Ingrid asked again.

"She…is," Myrtle said and hated the giggle that followed.

"To who?"

"Um…Percy Bledsoe, a lieutenant she met during the war at Fort McClellan."

"Poor Jake Green," Alice said. "He's been smitten with Rosemary since they were in school together. Of course, his mother will be relieved."

"His mother lost a wonderful chance at a daughter-in-law," Victoria said, unable to remain silent any longer. "Ava, would you please call the roll. Ladies, when you hear your name, please call out the flower you are most looking forward to planting this spring."

Ava began the roll call, and the discussion about Rosemary paused for the time being.

Chapter 16

Rosemary stooped down as she scrubbed the dingy floor, which was hard and cold to her bare knees. Michigan was much colder than Alabama. She dipped an old but clean sock in the mixture of water, vinegar, and lemon juice and then moved it back and forth with as much vigor as her arm would allow. The smell of vinegar made her pinch up her nose. She should have bought more than one lemon when Percy took her to the store. *Oh well, at least it will be clean!*

When she first saw the trailer Percy had rented for them the day before, she willed herself not to cry. It did give her something useful to do, however. By the time Percy got home from work, their new place would be pristine. If her mother had taught her anything growing up, it was how to pick cotton and how to properly clean.

She finished the floors and then sat down at one of the two kitchen chairs. The whole trailer consisted of their bedroom and a small kitchen. Tomorrow, she would begin cooking. She pulled out a sheet of paper to write to Ava first and then her parents and Judith. Ava's letter would be easier to write than the one to her parents. She looked over at the pocket watch Percy had left in the center of the table.

2:24, what would they all be doing at 2:24? Judith would be home from school by now and reluctantly helping her mother sweep the porch or hang up the washing or more like swing on

94

the washing when their mother wasn't watching. With it being Monday, Ava should be home from her morning classes and studying. *Does Edwin know yet? Did the shoes work?* It felt odd to be so misplaced and not know what her family was up to. She would have never dreamed that within one week and three days' time she would have left the only home she had ever known and be sitting in a trailer in northern Michigan. She suddenly felt lonelier than she had ever felt in her life. *Stop it! You chose this!*

She picked up a pen and began to write.

Dear Ava,
I am enjoying married life.

That much was true. Despite everything, she loved Percy, and he loved her. She just wished they could experience it closer to home.

Detroit is the biggest city I have ever seen. It seems funny to me now that I once thought Anniston was so big. There are men home from the war and people from all over the country come to work here. Percy started a job today at the Ford Motor Company assembling transmissions. Did you get a chance to talk to Mrs. Crockett? I wish I could have told her goodbye in person.

Rosemary stopped writing and looked down at her still hands. They were red and dry from all the scrubbing. When she made her hasty decision, she knew she would miss her family. She didn't expect to miss the store so much, though. *Who is making the night deposits now?*

Have you told anyone about your news yet? We met a woman from Mississippi the other day who had quadruplets! Can you imagine! No worries for you. You will have the cutest little boy or little girl alive. I need to write Mom and Dad now. Please write to me. I miss you all! I am putting our new address at the bottom of this letter.

Love,
Rosemary

Rosemary wrote a shorter letter to her parents and Judith and then started cleaning the kitchen. It came furnished. All the dishes and pans were well used but sturdy. She decided to scrub them all twice. Her hands were still in soap and water when Percy caught her by the waist.

"Have you been doing this all day?" He asked, removing the plate from her hand.

"Doesn't it all look better?" Rosemary said in return, and he glanced about the trailer. She could tell his day had been good by the confident spark of his brown eyes.

"Yes, but you know what looks even better?" He pulled her closer. "You and these lips I've been wanting to kiss all day."

He kissed her, and she hoped her water-logged hands weren't rough on his neck.

"How was work?" Rosemary asked when he released her.

"Not bad. Easy enough to get the hang of. I've got a surprise for you!" He sat down in one of the chairs and pulled her down on his lap.

"They're switching me to night shift starting tomorrow." He laughed when he felt her body tense.

"I'll be gone in the evenings, but we can sleep late in the mornings and spend all day together."

"Mornings together will be nice," she said and wondered what she would do each evening he was away.

"All right, then." He stood her up. "No work in the morning. So, dinner and dancing tonight."

"Tonight?"

"Why not Mrs. Bledsoe? Do you have somewhere else to be?"

"Only with you," she said before he kissed her again.

Chapter 17

Ava melted the butter and slowly poured in the milk as she stirred. She needed the top of her chicken pot pie to be perfect for what she must do. Tonight she would tell Edwin what she should have told him a month ago. The flour was next. She added it and then poured the paste over her dish of carrots, peas, potatoes, chicken, and broth. It was her husband's favorite meal that she cooked, and she would not disappoint. When it was in the oven, she paced the kitchen imagining the words she would use and their outcome.

"Edwin, you are going to be a father," she spoke to the empty air. "Edwin, we are going to have a new addition to our family."

She sighed and plopped down in her chair at the table. The words just didn't seem to fit her mouth or sound right once out.

"Well, it looks like Pete and Floraline aren't the only ones getting a fat baby," she tried again and laughed a startled laugh. *Maybe laughing isn't so bad. I wouldn't be crying. How much do babies weigh?*

She stood back up, and as she peeked in the oven to see if her crust was browning, she pretended to have a baby on her hip. It seemed like mothers were always doing house chores with babies propped on their side. *It sure won't be the most convenient way to get along!* She rubbed her abdomen. It didn't feel any bigger yet but she knew that would soon change. She had witnessed Floraline's transformation from the skinniest girl she knew to the most abundant girl she knew. *Will Edwin like me that way? I'll tell him right after dinner when his own belly is full and content.*

"There's just one place for me, near you. It's like to heaven to be near you," she sang. "Times when we're a part, I can't face my heart."

She would rather sing then think any more about babies or what life will or won't be like with them.

"Say you'll never stray more than just..." The front door unlatched, and she stopped singing. *He's home!*

She heard the thud of his work boots hitting the floor and then his quick steps to the kitchen. He knew where she would be and could smell the pie baking. Their eyes met, and he smiled. He looked sweaty and tired but happy to be home with her.

"Baby...we're having a baby." The words tumbled out of her mouth as if they couldn't be held back any longer.

"Did you say we're having a baby?"

"I'm so sorry." Her hands reached for the kitchen counter for support.

"Sorry for what?" He was by her side now, holding her hands with his calloused ones even though he had yet to bathe. "That's wonderful!"

"Do you really think so?" she said and felt her throat catch between tears and an absurd laugh.

"Yes!" He kissed her cheeks and then her lips. "I hope it's a girl. I want another one of you to love."

Ava exhaled as she felt the fear inside her change to joy. If he wanted it, she would want it.

Now for her family. Ava knew her mother would be ecstatic, and she was both ready for and dreaded the excitement she would be devoured with. Edwin wanted to tell them the moment the dishes were cleaned up, and it surprised her. Normally, he was so reserved about everything. Babies did strange things to people, though, and she supposed they were no different.

He held her hand and ushered her with an unaccustomed gentleness to her parents' house. *Maybe, I can get used to this kind of treatment!*

"Do you want to be the one to tell them?" she whispered, always afraid that Carson was in earshot.

"No, they would rather hear it from their daughter."

She breathed in the cool night air. He wanted them to know but he didn't want to have to say the words himself. She started to go through the various ways to tell them again in her head but stopped herself. None of it had mattered before. The words would come out one way or another.

They were now up the steps and at the door. Edwin kissed her again just before the door opened.

"Thought I heard you coming," Grandpa Chester said and moved aside for them.

"Oh, Ava, we were just coming to see you!" Victoria ran toward them. Something had happened. Her face told it all. It was the same excited look Ava had imagined after she told them their news.

"You'll never believe this!"

"She will," Sheffield said from behind his wife. "It's only the natural way of life."

"James and Vivie are having a baby!"

Ava's face fell, and she gripped Edwin's hand. The touch of her hand told him everything. They would not be telling anyone else tonight.

"Oh, sweetie, I didn't think about you being afraid for Vivie." Victoria pulled her daughter into her arms. "What happened to our poor Estelle won't happen to Vivie. That sort of thing is rare these days. Don't you worry. We'll pray for her every day, and God will give us a new baby for our family to love."

Chapter 18

"Make my life worthwhile by telling me that I'll spend the rest of my days, all of those happy, happy days…so near you," Ava sang and then listened as the song faded and ended without her.

Willie Harold's baton dropped, and the room was as quiet as it had been noisy a moment ago.

"That's a wrap," Willie said. "I think that was about as perfect as you can get."

"What did you expect?" one of the bassoon players retorted, and they all laughed.

"Now, for some news that I think will excite you all." Everyone was quiet again. "We'll be traveling a little further for our next performance. We've been asked to perform at the Georgian Terrace Hotel Easter weekend and…" Willie paused for the chatter that followed his announcement, and Ava's heart beat faster. Her audience was once again expanding.

"If the name Georgian Terrace Hotel sounds familiar," Willie spoke again, a little louder than before, "it's because it's the hotel right across from the Fox Theatre. We'll be playing in the same ballroom where the *Gone with the Wind* gala was held."

More murmurs of excitement swept from mouth to mouth, and Ava couldn't wait to carry the news home.

"Ava, do you mind a bigger stage?" Willie turned to her.

"Of course not!"

The bus back to Jacksonville was more than half full, and it seemed as though everyone on it had something to talk about. Ava leaned back in her seat and gazed out the window. It was all just a background buzz. Her mind was in a ballroom she had never seen about a hundred miles away. Her ruby lips spread in a smile as she imagined the grand room that Vivien Leigh and Clark Gable and Carole Lombard had once sat in. White marble and massive chandeliers gleamed in her mind. It was hard to believe that she would be singing in that very room. A dull pain in her abdomen distracted her thoughts. She massaged it for a moment and then crossed her hands in her lap, not wanting anyone to see the gesture. No one seemed to be paying her any attention, and she gazed back out at the tree tops. Some were showing off new leaves and that made her happy too. She hated being cold and was ready for spring. Another dull pain. This time it felt like it was also in her lower back. She sat up taller, hoping she wasn't starting to get sick like Estelle did when she was pregnant. She didn't feel nauseous at all, though. If anything, she was hungry again. *Could this be pregnancy hunger pains?*

The rest of the ride was uncomfortable, and she couldn't wait to get off the bus. By the time she got home, the pain had escalated, and she lay bunched up on the couch. She was still lying that way when Edwin found her.

"Feeling puny?" he asked as he sat down on one side of the couch and lifted her feet into his lap.

"Afraid so," she said. "Sorry about dinner. We'll just eat at Mom's tonight." She wasn't hungry anymore.

"Ava!" Edwin screamed at her. "You're bleeding!"

She sat up and saw the red stains seeping through her yellow dress.

"Are you ok?"

"I don't know. Go get Mom!"

He was out the door in a moment, and she was left crying and clutching her stomach as the pain returned.

Ava felt like she was back in time but somehow reversed in the story. Her mother was bent over her, wiping her cheeks and brow with a warm, wet cloth the same way she had treated Estelle just a few years ago.

"It's going to be alright," Victoria said in the soothing, almost musical way she had of speaking to sick people. "Many women have miscarriages and go on to have healthy children. I know you'll mourn this one, but Jesus will take care of him or her for you."

Ava choked back more tears. Something, someone had died inside of her.

"Why didn't you tell me?" Victoria spoke in a lower voice as she now smoothed back her daughter's hair.

Ava just looked at her mother, not sure of how to put all of her old and new feelings into words.

"Have you been afraid because of what happened to Estelle?"

Ava nodded. Edwin hadn't guessed the truth, but her mother knew.

"I see. God has different plans for us all. We must trust and not fear."

Her tears could not be choked back now. What if her fear had killed her baby, Edwin's baby? Victoria pulled her up into her arms and held her as she cried.

Chapter 19

"Don't look at me like that. It'll be good for you." Percy lifted up Rosemary's chin with the bend of his finger.

"How am I supposed to spend the entire evening alone with someone I've never met?" Rosemary replied, arms crossed.

"You're girls. How hard can it be?" he asked and then laughed as she grunted and turned away from him.

"If we have to eat together, what do I serve her? I wasn't expecting company."

Percy laughed again and turned her back toward him. He uncrossed her arms and wrapped them around himself instead.

"She's from South Carolina. I'm sure she'll like your banana sandwiches."

She looked up at him, and he could detect a smile starting to upturn her mouth. He could always bring her around to his way of thinking.

"Come on, Rosemary. Give her a try. It's not good for you to by yourself every night."

There was no more time to argue. Someone was knocking at their door. They pulled away from each other, and Rosemary smoothed down her skirt and tucked her hair behind her ears. It was getting so long and unmanageable.

"Hi Johnny. Hi Annamae," Percy greeted. He waved them inside the trailer and reached back for his wife's hand.

"Wow, so clean!" Annamae spoke first, taking off her coat and dropping it on one of the kitchen chairs. She was short and pudgy with a round, welcoming face, a bob of red hair, and redder lips than Ava dared.

"Rosemary spends too much time cleaning." Percy pulled Rosemary forward. "Hopefully, you can keep her from it tonight. This place is so small that it doesn't need anymore."

"Nice to meet you," Johnny said and nodded toward her. He was much taller than his wife, but with his freckled face and crew cut hair, he looked like a boy in a man's pants.

"You too," Rosemary replied.

"We need to be heading out. You two have fun." Percy kissed her full on the mouth, and Rosemary blushed, embarrassed to be kissed in front of two people she had just met.

They were soon out the door, and she and Annamae were left looking at each other. Annamae started laughing, and Rosemary laughed too not knowing what else to do.

"Sorry to be dropped on you," Annamae said.

"Would you like something to drink?" Rosemary offered, wishing again that she had been told soon enough to prepare something.

"Not just yet." Annamae sat down at the table. "How do you like Detroit?"

"It's so big and busy," Rosemary answered and sat down across from her.

"Wish I could bring my mom and pop up here for a visit. They wouldn't know what to think. All sorts of different people shopping together, eating together, and working together."

"We've met people from just about everywhere too."

"My brother said New York was the same way."

"Does he live there?"

"Not now. He died in the war."

"I'm so sorry," Rosemary said, thinking she shouldn't ask any more questions.

"Thank you." Annamae smiled to show she didn't mind the question. "We're all learning how to get along with it. I've got another brother, Charlie, and a sister, Nan, who still live near mom and pop. They, well my other brother, is a comfort to them. My sister just stirs up trouble, though. Married to one man in the Army. Divorced him as soon as he got home from the war. Said she never really knew him. Just married him to give a good time before he left. Can you imagine! My mom was beside herself. Doesn't know what to say to the poor man's mother at church! Now Nan is just about to marry the old town butcher of all people. Mom is furious. Thinks Nan just wants to give him a good time before he dies too."

"Is that so?" Rosemary replied before Annamae began telling her about how the butcher was a very fat man and in bad health. At least she didn't have to talk much.

When their stomachs began to growl, Rosemary made them banana sandwiches on white bread with mayonnaise. She cut the banana slices thick, and Annamae said that was just the way her grandmother used to eat them but with a little peanut butter too.

"Want a cigarette?" Annamae asked when they had finished their sandwiches. She pulled out a box of Chesterfields from her purse.

Rosemary just looked at them. Her mother had always told her that smoking was for men and that ladies didn't smoke. Almost all the women she had seen out in Detroit smoked, however, and some of them had to be ladies.

"I'll try one."

"Never smoked before?"

"No."

"It's relaxing. Did I tell you that the butcher has never been married before?"

"No," Rosemary replied as Annamae lit her cigarette.

"We've tried to tell Nan that there is something in that, but she refuses to listen."

Rosemary smoked, coughed, and listened to Annamae tell her family tales the rest of the night. She had to admit it was more fun than being by herself another night.

Chapter 20

Ava let whoever was on her porch knock three times before she made herself get out of bed and go to the door. She didn't feel like company. It was probably either her mother or Myrtle with more stories about other women who miscarried and words about "carrying on." She now knew that her aunt Elizabeth had miscarried once and Myrtle, herself, had miscarried three times between Rosemary and Judith. Why they thought her knowing all of this would be of any comfort she didn't have the least idea. She didn't want to know about other babies dying before they were born or that it could occur to her more than once. The door swung open with an angry push, and Carson stood on the other side. He was holding two Hershey chocolate bars and a bottle of Coca Cola. *Did they tell him too of all people?* He gave her a half smile out of one corner of his mouth. Becoming a pastor had softened him even toward her.

"Here," he said, holding out the chocolate bars and drink. "Mom said you've been feeling poorly."

"Thank you," she muttered. She opened up one of the bars and handed him the other.

"They're both for you."

"Just take it," she said, thumping him on the chest with the unopened bar. He took it, and they sat down together on the couch. She couldn't remember the last time she had been alone with him.

"Haven't been getting out much?" he asked.

"Haven't felt like it," she replied as the chocolate sweetened her tongue. It was good to feel something.

"Are your teachers all right with you missing so many classes?"

"When you're sick, you're sick," she said, unable to keep the anger she felt at herself and what had happened out of her tone. She had missed two weeks of classes and band rehearsals, and she hadn't cared until that moment. "What's been going on with you?"

"Just the usual. Oh, I baptized a whole family in the river last Sunday."

"That must have been something," she said, remembering how her mom said that her baby was with Jesus now and she need not worry. *Should I ask Carson?*

"Nice family. They live out near the grist mill in Heflin."

"What's this I hear about soybeans and Mom?" Ava asked instead.

"Dad and I are trying to talk her into replacing a part of our cotton crop with soybeans. Pete Gunter suggested it, and we don't think it's a bad idea. Mom doesn't think so at all though."

"What about Grandpa?"

"It doesn't matter to him one way or the other. As long as he has his buttermilk and cornbread every night, he says to do as we see fit."

"Want some milk or tea?" Ava asked. The chocolate had to be making him thirsty.

"Milk."

They moved to the kitchen, and Ava poured him a glass.

"Still got a checkers board here?"

"Why, feel like getting beat?" She smiled despite everything.

"We'll see who does the beating!"

Later that night, Carson lay on his back on the hay-strewn barn floor. It was where he prepared all his sermons and did his serious praying. He had a mental list of prayer needs from his small congregation. Mrs. Duncan had the shingles. The Faulkners were grieving the loss of a nephew. Otis Nunn was feuding with his brother. He would pray for them all, but his own sister was coming first tonight.

"Dear Lord, please bless Ava. Please renew her strength, her faith, and her joy."

The next morning, Ava was back at the Jacksonville State Teachers College surrounded by a classroom of girls her age, many unmarried but some married like herself.

"Are you going to the spring dance?" A girl named Viola asked from behind her.

"If I can talk Donald into taking me," another girl named Miriam answered. "He would rather do anything than dance."

"Has anyone seen a white pearl earring? I seem to have lost one," someone else asked.

Ava didn't turn around to see who had lost the earring. She felt different inside now, like she had been pulled away from their world.

112

"Ava, I copied down my Music Appreciation notes for you for the test tomorrow," Rebekah said from beside her.

"Thank you," Ava replied and took the notes from her.

"Was it the flu? My mom says the flu is going around again?"

"I don't think so, but I felt rotten," Ava told the truth as best as she could.

"Umm, Umm," Mrs. Wheeler cleared her throat, walking to her place at the front of the classroom. "Time to quiet down and get to work. Ava, good to have you back. We'll have you all caught up in no time."

Ava mustered another smile for her teacher, but her body yearned for the solitude and stillness of her bed.

Chapter 21

Annamae was talking again. Her parents had told her sister that her second marriage shouldn't be in the same church where she married her first husband, and another uproar had ensued. Nan was threatening to just elope, and Annamae wished she would and save everyone the bother.

"Sometimes, I'm relieved to be so far away from it all," she said. "And other times I just wish I was there to speak my mind in person."

Rosemary nodded along, but she was having trouble listening. Ava's most recent letter was still fresh on her mind. *A miscarriage, how could that have happened!* She felt guilty being away from her cousin. Unlike Annamae, she wanted desperately to be there.

"Cigarette?" Annamae offered, lighting her own.

"No, thank you," Rosemary replied. She had decided that she would leave smoking to the men as her mother advised. They made her sick to her stomach.

The front door opened, and their husbands were back hours before they were expected.

"What are you doing back so early?" Annamae asked for them.

"Didn't have a choice," Johnny said as Rosemary searched Percy's face for an answer.

She could tell he was disturbed, and she reached for his hand.

"They let us go," Percy explained, taking her hand. "Well, not exactly. The workers at the Ford plant have gone on strike, so there is no work to be done while things are being sorted out."

"How long could that take?" Annamae asked.

"Who knows? A week, a month, months," Percy answered.

"We'll find something else in the meantime," Johnny said.

"Sure, there are all kinds of jobs in this city." Percy smiled, convincing them all to smile too. "Nothing more to be done tonight. Let's go out!"

"Do you feel like that?" Rosemary spoke up.

"Why not? Better to have fun with you than mope here." He picked her up and spun her around.

Soon, Percy was spinning her again but on a crowded danced floor. His shirt was halfway unbuttoned, and his hands felt hot against hers. She smiled up at him, determined to be happy with him despite the unforeseen strike. He smiled back and kissed her again, tasting of the alcohol he had been drinking. She was still trying to get used to him kissing her in public.

"I see a guy I know from the plant. Give me just a minute," he spoke in her ear and led her to an empty space next to the wall.

"Go," she said back over the music. She watched him shake hands with the man. A new song was starting, and her eyes wandered to the stage. She had never seen a black band perform before, and they had an energy that the Willie Harold Band didn't. Ava would have loved the performance.

"You reach your destination, but alas and alack! You need some compensation to get back in the black," the lead singer sang out. "You take your morning paper from the top of the stack. And read the situation from the front to the back. The only job that's open needs a man with a knack, so put it right back in the rack, Jack!"

Rosemary tapped her foot to the beat and watched Annamae's red bob bounce and up and down as she laughed and danced with Johnny.

"Choo choo, choo choo, ch'boogie! Woo woo, ooh ooh, ch'boogie!" the music continued. Percy was still talking with the man, another drink in his hand.

The song ended, and the next one took its place.

"Sorry," Percy said, back by her side. "Got some job leads."

"Good! Want to dance some more?" The music was overcoming even her normal inhibitions.

"Yes, I do." He laughed at her and allowed her to lead him back onto the dance floor. They danced in a fast, feverish manner like the music, but something about Percy's almost maniac moves began to temper Rosemary's mood.

Chapter 22

The bus ride home was as noisy as it had been the last time, but Ava was glad of it.

"Tell me the ingredients for that recipe again?" she heard a woman ask behind her. The person she was speaking to was soft spoken, and a man two rows ahead of her drowned out the list of ingredients.

"The Rams are looking good at practice. Could be another league title for Anniston," he said.

She listened to snippets of various conversations about cooking and baseball and parenting trying to forget the horrible band practice she was returning from. The band had learned two new songs in her absence, and she had struggled to keep up. They all expressed concern over her recent bad health, and Willie told her that her voice was as clear and pretty as always, but it wasn't. She felt as though her mouth were disconnected from her body and singing unintelligible words from a sheet of paper. *How will I get through that again next week?*

An expected lurch shifted everyone forward in their seat, and Ava stood up to get off at her usual stop.

"Have a good day, miss," the bus driver said, and Ava smiled.

"You too."

No sooner had her feet reached the ground than her parents were by her side, her mother clutching her hand.

"What's wrong?" Ava asked as they ushered her away from the bus and to the car, which sat just off the road.

"There's been an accident at the foundry," Sheffield said, and his daughter's body went limp. "Edwin was burned badly, but he's at Anniston Memorial Hospital. That's all we know." He half carried her the rest of the way to the car.

The smell was the first thing Ava noticed. She had never been in a hospital before. Everything looked white and sterile from the nurse's clothing to the walls to the beds she spotted through the half-closed doors they passed, but there was an odor that couldn't be ignored. It was the smell of unhealthiness muddled by cleaners and flowers. She wanted to pinch her nose, but her parents had her by both hands as she trembled her way to Edwin's room. She couldn't speak until she had seen him.

"This is your husband and son-in-law's room." A nurse halted them outside a closed door. "Just let me have a word with the doctor."

Sheffield steadied his daughter with his gentle eyes, and Victoria squeezed her hand as they waited impatiently. After a few minutes, the nurse re-opened the door and waved them in. Edwin was lying in a bed covered in a blanket except for part of his upper body. Another nurse was dressing his arm while a bearded man in a white coat studied an exposed area on his chest. The doctor turned when he heard them.

"Hello, Mrs. Livingston." He reached out his hand, and Ava somehow managed to shake it. "Mr. and Mrs. Stilwell, I believe." Sheffield and Victoria also shook hands with the doctor. "I'm Dr. Boland."

Edwin now knew they were there as well, and he turned his head to find Ava.

"I'm so sorry," he said when he had found her. His eyes were red and feral, the way they were often when she first met him. What caught her attention next were the white, waxy spots surrounded by black, charred skin on his chest.

She shook her head in response, unable to speak for her tears.

"He was burned by molten metal," the doctor informed them. "It splattered him on his chest and left arm."

"How bad are the burns?" Sheffield asked.

"I'm afraid they are third degree burns. His tissue is quite damaged, and I think some of his nerves are as well. We've given him morphine, but his pain has been limited because of the nerve damage. We'll keep him awhile to treat and dress the wounds. His body temperature is also low, so we need to treat him for possible hypothermia as well."

"Can I stay with him?" Ava asked, her voice barely perceptible.

"We can have a chair brought in for you, but it's important that your husband not move or be startled. He was in shock when they brought him in."

"I can stay as well," Victoria said.

"I think one guest is all that is recommended in his condition."

"Of course. We'll stay close by then."

Late that night when the nurses had left and the room was dark, Ava left her chair in the corner and went to Edwin's bed. She found his right hand underneath the blanket and held it. He was cold, and she decided to ask the nurse about more blankets.

119

"I love you," she whispered.

"I'll heal," Edwin whispered back. "I'm so sorry to trouble you this way, especially now."

"This wasn't your fault. It's what I was afraid might happen every day you left for work, but it's not your fault. We'll heal together," she said, and they each cried for the other and the baby who was lost to them.

When the patient returned home, Victoria was able to be as "close by" as she wanted.

"Be sure to secure the bandage like the doctor showed us," she said to her daughter who was redressing a burn on her husband's upper arm.

"You don't have to fuss so much over me," Edwin said.

"We most certainly do," Victoria replied. "Do you want this arm to fall off from infection or do you want to get better?"

"Get better, of course. I just hate to see you both worry…"

"Nonsense. We'll quit fussing over you when you're out of this bed."

Ava finished with the last of the fresh bandages.

"Do you want a drink of water or anything?" she asked.

"No, not right now."

"I think what you need the most now is sleep," Victoria said. "Best medicine. Gives the body time to heal without being bothered."

"All right then," Edwin replied. He hadn't been sleeping well, and if he was sleeping, they wouldn't have to attend to him for a while.

"Call me if you need anything." Ava stood up from the side of their bed and tried to smile at him. The sight of him lying there so helpless still made her cry.

"Ava, come on. I'll help you take down your wash." Victoria nudged her.

"Thank you both," Edwin said.

"No more thank yous are necessary."

Victoria led Ava out of the patient's room and onto the porch. For the last few days, she had not only been helping out with treating Edwin's burns but also with her daughter's housework. Ava didn't remonstrate, knowing it would be a waste of words.

"Before we get the wash, I want to talk to you." Victoria sat down on the bottom step and stretched out her short legs. She patted the place on the step next to her, and Ava sat down reluctantly. She would have rather just gone and gotten the wash. Anytime her mother wanted to stop everything and talk, it wasn't pleasant for the other person.

"You've been moping around the last several weeks, and I've let you. Losing a baby and seeing your husband get injured gives you a right to mope a little, but enough is enough. What that man needs now more than anything is a joyful wife. Life hurts sometimes. That's just all there is to it. Now you're going to get back to living and let that man in there do the same. No more skipping classes or practices. I'll take care of Edwin when you're gone."

"But I don't want to leave him."

"It won't be for long each day, and he doesn't want you to give up everything that you've worked so hard for."

They sat in silence for a moment, and Ava decided that since Rosemary wasn't there she would tell her mother what had been troubling her the most.

"I'm afraid my fear killed that baby," she said, looking down at the dusty ground in the afternoon light.

"Why would you think such a thing?"

"I've heard you say before that fear and worry can work misery on a body. What if it damaged…"

"Don't ever let me hear you say that again! Nothing you did caused that baby to miscarry."

Ava sighed and dared to look up at her mother.

"I'll try to be happy for him."

"Good, now let's get that wash in before it rains."

Ava followed her mother out to the clothesline. The sky was beginning to look rather gray and disgruntled.

Chapter 23

"Now can you tell me where we're going?" Rosemary asked as Percy turned off a busy street full of shops, businesses, and restaurants and onto a more residential one lined with quaint, old houses.

"I'll tell you when we get there. Don't spoil your surprise."

He drove the car with one hand and held her hand with the other. It was the happiest she had seen him in weeks. He now had a job with the Bundy Corporation making refrigerator parts, and he was earning more money than he had with Ford.

They pulled up to a two-story, gray and white house surrounded by a few trees on either side. The trees took Rosemary's attention more than the house. She loved trees and had seen little of them since moving to Detroit. In a couple of months, the warmer weather would make them more to look at, but to her, they were still beautiful, bare and all.

"Welcome to your new home!" Percy said.

"My new home?" She pulled her eyes away from the trees to his face.

"Well, just the upper floor. The Ramseys own the house, but they rent out their second floor."

"I don't know what to say."

"No more drafty trailer. Doesn't this look more like a home?"

"Yes!" She squeezed his hand.

"One day we'll own a whole house just like this one."

"With lots of trees," Rosemary added, and he laughed at her.

"Come on. Let's go inside."

The porch was long and reminded her of home. A swing was at one end, and large rectangular windows were on either side of the door. She could see a piano and a table with a white, lace doily and a lamp through the window closest to her. Percy knocked, and a much older man opened the door.

"Hello, Percy. Ready to move in?"

"We sure are," Percy said, shaking hands with their new landlord. "This is my wife Rosemary."

"How do you do?" Rosemary said, admiring the man's white hair. It was the whitest hair she had ever seen.

"Fine, just fine. Eloise, they're here!" he called.

An older woman wearing glasses and an apron joined them.

"So wonderful to meet you, dear."

Rosemary held out her hand but was hugged by the older woman instead.

"And you as well."

"It'll be so nice to have some young ones in the house again." Mrs. Ramsey hugged Percy next. "Let's show you around the old place."

"Certainly," Mr. Ramsey said and led them to the big open room just to the right of the door. "Our living area."

Rosemary took it all in, the piano she had seen from outside, two chairs, a sofa, a table, a bookcase with a large radio sitting on top, and dozens of framed, mostly unsmiling people hanging on the walls and sitting about.

"You have so many pictures," she said.

"Yes, yes," Mr. Ramsey answered. "I come from a very large family. You'll have to sit and let Mrs. Ramsey tell you about them all."

"You would find it rather entertaining," Mrs. Ramsey agreed. "Thomas has quite a number of hooligans in his line of descent."

Percy and Rosemary laughed and continued their tour to the dining room, which contained the formal dining table and a china cabinet, and then to the kitchen.

"Anytime you want to fix something to eat, the kitchen is yours," Mrs. Ramsey said. She had obviously been in the middle of making some kind of bread. A ball of dough set in a circle of flour on the counter.

"Thank you," Rosemary said. "I haven't gotten to cook much since moving to Detroit." In truth, Percy preferred to dine out.

"Well, it's here for you anytime."

They finished the downstairs rooms and were escorted to their new rooms upstairs. They had two bedrooms and a bathroom. They would sleep in the larger bedroom and use the second one for storage or extra seating. In the second room, a rocking chair sat by a square window overlooking the porch and a rather quiet street despite all the commercial activity just a few blocks away. The Ramseys left them to settle in, and they quickly unpacked the small amount of things they had brought with them. When they were done, Percy stretched out on their new bed, and Rosemary lay down next to him.

"Can you be happy here?" he asked.

"Of course. Can you?"

"I'd be happy anywhere with you."

She laughed at his answer, and he pulled her closer.

"Oh, I have a favor to ask of you tomorrow. Would you mail this for me?"

He pulled out an envelope from his front shirt pocket and handed it to her. It was addressed to his son in care of his former wife. Rosemary's heart swelled. She had been praying for weeks that he would reach out to his son.

"Just a note letting him know our new address and a small amount of money to help out with clothes and things. Probably won't make much of a difference, but there it is."

Rosemary kissed him on the cheek. She was more proud of him than she had ever been.

"It will make a difference," she said. "It always makes a difference when you know someone cares about you."

He grinned at her optimism and then kissed her.

Early the next morning, they tiptoed together down the stairs to the kitchen. Percy worked day shift now, and they didn't want to disturb the Ramseys. Mrs. Ramsey had made room for some of their groceries in her refrigerator. Back home, they still used ice boxes to keep foods cool, and Rosemary was astonished at how cold their eggs were when she took them out of the Kelvinator-brand refrigerator.

"Never seen eggs before," Percy whispered in her ear and laughed.

"Not this cold," she replied and placed the eggs in his hands.

"Astounding!" He grinned at her. She took the eggs back from him, and they both laughed as they found a skillet and fried their eggs for breakfast. They sat down at the smaller table in the kitchen to eat.

"I'll leave you money for the trolley. You can shop and get something for lunch," Percy said.

"I'm going to mail your letter and then come straight home today."

"Why? Mrs. Ramsey had the place clean before you stepped foot in it."

"I know, but I need to make the rooms my own."

"I'll leave you plenty of money in case you change your mind."

They finished their breakfast, and Percy left for work. It was Rosemary's first day all to herself in weeks. No Percy looking for a job and taking her out all the time, and no Annamae talking nonstop. She sat in the rocking chair by the window and wrote letters to her parents and Ava, describing what she knew so far of the house, the Ramseys, the refrigerator, the cold eggs, and the street outside her window.

Chapter 24

Carson laid down his Bible on the wooden, cross-shaped pulpit and looked out at his small congregation. There were two visitors today. His sister and his brother-in-law sat on the last pew. None of his family had heard him preach in a while, and it was good to have them in his church again. He knew why Ava was there, though. She hadn't been in church since her misfortune and the accident, unwilling to face those who knew her best yet. He just hoped he could say something that would help.

"And seeing the multitudes, he went up into a mountain, and when he was set, his disciples came unto him, and he opened his mouth and taught them, saying: Blessed are the poor in spirit, for theirs is the kingdom of heaven," he read Matthew 5:1-3 and then paused. "When I first read these words as a child, I thought, 'Who wants to be poor in spirt? I want to be rich in spirit.' Poor in spirit means, however, that we should be humble and recognize our need for God when we come before Him, and let's face it, we all need Him."

He paused again, his blue eyes surveying the small crowd.

"Amen," Deacon Faulkner let out in a reverent voice.

"That takes us to our next verse. 'Blessed are they that mourn, for they shall be comforted.' I've been your pastor for a couple of years now, and I've seen you mourn. The war affected us all. Many of you lost loved ones. We all face difficulty, sickness, and death, and I personally don't see how anyone does it without God. Jesus didn't say blessed are those who mourn for you will not mourn again. He said blessed are those who mourn for I will comfort them. That's His promise for us today, and it's a good one. David wrote in Psalms 46:1, 'God is our refuge and strength, a very present help in trouble.'"

Carson chanced a glance at his sister. She was listening, eyes on him and not out the window as she often did at their home church. She also wasn't smirking the way she usually did when she heard him preach, unable to take her older brother seriously. Instead, her face was focused as she sat by her healing husband.

"Blessed are the meek, for they shall inherit the earth," Carson moved on through the beatitudes and finished his sermon. The church's music minister then took the pulpit, and everyone picked up their hymnals to sing.

"When peace like a river attendeth my soul, when sorrow like sea billows roll. Whatever my lot, Thou hast taught me to say, 'It is well. It is well with my soul,'" they all sang out in unison, and Carson paced before the altar praying over his sister, brother-in-law, and congregation.

The service ended, and Ava and Edwin waited while Carson spoke to the line of church members leaving for Sunday lunch.

"Excellent sermon today, Reverend Stilwell," Mr. Duncan said and shook Carson's hand.

"I hope it touched some hearts," Carson replied.

"Come and eat with us next Sunday," Mrs. Duncan said next when it was her turn to shake their pastor's hand goodbye.

"That's very sweet of you, Mrs. Duncan, but my mother will want me home for Easter lunch."

"Well, do think about reconsidering. I have a niece I want you to meet. She might be just the one God has for you!"

"You're very thoughtful, but I'm in no hurry to get married," Carson replied as kindly as possible. The older women were always trying to play matchmaker for him, and he was determined to put an end to it. Someone always had a daughter or a niece or a relative to introduce him too. He hoped that Ava hadn't heard her request.

When all the people had filed out of the church, Carson drove them home in the car James had given him.

"I think you should go eat lunch with Mrs. Duncan and her niece next week, Rev. Stilwell," Ava leaned forward from where she sat alone in the back seat and said to her brother.

"Just stop it," he replied as she laughed.

"Why don't you come to Altanta with us next weekend instead?"

"And miss Easter service with my church?"

"Why not? I'm sure another pastor could take your place one Sunday."

"I don't think so."

"It'll be fun. I could get you into the ballroom. God didn't say preachers can't dance."

"This preacher doesn't."

"James and Vivie are coming, and we're staying with them afterwards. They would love to see you."

"Not this time."

"Ella would love to see you too." At this, Carson did seem to ponder the opportunity.

"Still a no. Edwin, you ready to go back to work?"

"Yep, I feel useless at the house," he answered truthfully.

"He wouldn't be if they hadn't found him a carpentry position." Ava leaned forward again and dangled her arms over the front seat between them.

"Alright, we know how you feel," Edwin said to his wife. "I'll be a pattern maker now making wooden molds for the cast iron."

"Sounds like a better job," Carson said.

"No more hot metal ever again!" Ava exclaimed, and Carson and Edwin laughed, but Edwin's still stinging burns made him agree with his wife. He would never have complete use of his left arm again.

Chapter 25

Ava sat in her chair just to the right of the band, waiting for her turn to sing and looking out over the glistening ballroom. It was as grand as she had imagined with majestic columns, crystal chandeliers, and a large dance floor encircled by white-clothed tables decorated with bouquets of Easter lilies. With the band, she had performed at many places and on radio, but this was the best so far. She half expected some of the hotel's most famous guests to appear at any moment. Rudolph Valentino, Olivia de Havilland, Margaret Mitchell, Walt Disney - her mind spun thinking of how they had all been in the room in which she was about to sing. None of Hollywood's elite tonight, but there were plenty of Atlanta dignitaries dancing and dining to their music. The Georgian Terrace was rightly known as Atlanta's "Paris hotel."

One couple dancing was James and Vivie, and despite her obvious pregnancy, Vivie was swaying to the music just as much as anyone else in the room. Ava wondered if the baby was enjoying being bounced here and there. Her mother would definitely disapprove of dancing while with child, and Ava decided she would leave that part out of her evening's description to her mother. Vivie did look attractive, though. So many women she knew changed for the worse during pregnancy but not her sister-in-law. She wore a floral print taken out at the waist but still tight against her bosom and shoulders. Her hair was chin length now and pinned up on both sides. James still looked happy by her side. She assumed he was glad about the baby. A wave of nausea overcame her as she realized that she would have looked much like Vivie tonight if she hadn't lost her baby. The thought turned her eyes upon her husband. He sat at the far back table waiting for her exit from the stage. There would be no dancing for them tonight. The movement would still be too painful for him. She had barely been able to touch him since his injury.

"Ava," the horn player next to her whispered. "You're up!"

Ava made her way quickly to the center of the stage and stepped behind the mic just as Willie nodded at her and the chorus began.

"You made me love you. I didn't want to do it. I didn't want to do it. You made me want you, and all the time you knew it. I guess you always knew it." Ava's voice filled the ballroom. "You made me happy. Sometimes, you made me glad, but there were times, dear, you made me feel so bad."

When the song finished and the band continued without her, she joined Edwin.

"Isn't this place beautiful?" she asked.

"I don't know. I've just been watching my Songbird. She's the beautiful one," he replied and put his good arm around her.

"You're silly!"

Vivie plopped down on Edwin's other side.

"Ok, I'm going to give this baby a minute to rest!" she said.

"Then I'm going to dance with my little sis." James pulled Ava up out of her seat. An up-tempo jump number had just begun.

"Go on!" Vivie shooed them away with her hands.

Ava followed her older brother onto the dance floor and the let the music take her over. James had always been a good dancer, and he had learned some new moves with Vivie. It was exhilarating to feel so free and abandoned. They danced until they were both breathless and the band needed her back.

"Knock another one out of the park," James said to her as she rushed back on stage. She had already almost missed one song! Something about the hotel and the ambience and the music was making her forget everything, and it felt good.

Ella's face was the first thing Ava saw when they arrived at James and Vivie's house late that night. Instead of staying with the band, she and Edwin were staying the night with James. Ava was glad to be with her brother and didn't mind missing a chance to spend the night at a hotel after the Winecoff disaster.

"Auntie, auntie," Ella called, and Ava took her up in her arms. Even in the short time between Christmas and Easter, her niece looked less like a baby and more like a little girl.

"What is she doing up?" Ava heard James whisper to Vivie behind her.

"What did you expect? Of course she would want to see Ava."

"Whenever did you learn to say auntie?" Ava asked, ignoring the conversation behind her.

"Elijah's been teaching her all sorts of words," Vivie said.

"She can say about anything." Vivie's seven year-old brother appeared. Like Vivie, he was blond and grinning.

"Ava, Edwin, this is Elijah, my youngest brother, and my mother, Ruth."

"So nice to meet you," Ava said, and Edwin nodded from beside her.

"We've been wanting to meet Vivie's new family," Ruth said. She was a small woman with light, greying hair. "Hopefully, your parents can come over for a visit before too much longer."

"They would like that. Ella, what else can you say?"

"Froggie, shoe, candy," the little girl said, and they all laughed.

"Don't tell your mother, Ava, but I think she probably has a little too much of the last of those thanks to my brothers," Vivie admitted.

"It's not my fault!" Elijah stomped his foot. "Ernest and Gordon are the ones who keep buying it for her with their paper route money."

"Some candy won't hurt her," Ava said and hugged her niece closer. How she had missed that soft skin and little laugh.

"James, why don't you go ahead and drive Mom and Elijah home," Vivie said. "I'll get Ava and Edwin settled in, and we can put Ella to bed."

"Of course," James replied.

"Tell your daddy goodnight, Ella."

"Goodnigh…" Ella said without the "t," and Ava's heart sank at the way the light in her niece's amber eyes dimmed when she looked toward her father.

"Goodnight," James called back from the other side of the door, and Ava was ashamed of him. Their father had always ruffled their hair and kissed them on the head when they were little children going to bed for the night.

"Ella, can you show Ava and Edwin your room," Vivie said. "They get to sleep in your bed tonight, and you get to sleep with me and daddy."

"My room!" Ella squealed when Ava put her down. She took off as soon as her feet hit the floor, and Ava and Edwin laughed as they followed her.

The room where she led them was filled with pink, white, and yellow curtains, bedding, doll clothes, and girl clothes.

"Ella, I love your room!" Ava said, wishing her mother could see it too. If James had done one thing right, it was finding Vivie.

"My mother and grandma are quite the seamstresses," Vivie said. "They've helped me make all sorts of things for Ella."

"Wish I had a trunk full of doll clothes when I was growing up!"

"We did out do ourselves on the doll clothes. Fun to make and a good way to use up scrap cloth pieces." Vivie sat down on Ella's bed and rubbed her belly. "I do hope that Ella will have a baby sister to play with soon."

"Unca." Ella placed one of her dolls in Edwin's hand. "Play."

"Thank you," he said and pretended to kiss Ella's cheek with the doll.

"Ella would play dolls with you all night if we'd let her," Vivie said and let out one of her loud laughs. "Hope this bed is not too small for you two."

"We'll be fine," Ava said.

A short while later, however, when they were alone in the room, Ava wasn't so sure.

"Edwin, I can sleep on the floor. I don't want to hurt you," she offered. She had been sleeping on the couch since his accident.

"I'm tired of being away from you," he said. "Lay against my good side."

"What if I accidently bump your chest or your arm in my sleep?"

"I'll live. I want my wife back."

"I've never left you," she said and unfastened her pale pink gown.

"But you have kept your distance."

"For your own good. Not because I wanted to!"

"You know, I think that's my favorite of your dresses," he said, watching her take off the gown.

"It's definitely my fanciest dress." Ava left on her slip and climbed into bed next to him. She gently let her body slide up against his.

"It's nice to touch you again," she said, and he kissed her.

Edwin was quickly asleep, but Ava was so afraid of hurting of him that she couldn't get comfortable. Tired of trying, she decided to find a drink of water. Edwin grunted when she got up but didn't wake. She tiptoed out the door and to the kitchen. The light was on, and her brother was at the table with several books and papers spread out around him.

"What are you doing up at this time of night?"

He jumped when she spoke.

"You could let a person know when you're coming!" He laid down his pencil and rubbed his eyes with the backs of his hands. "Studying. Can't study during the day like you can. Too many classes, work things, and family things."

"So, you think it's easy for me," she said and sat down at the chair across from him.

"Easier. What are you doing up?"

"Couldn't get to sleep. Thought I would get a drink of water."

"I think we have that." He left the table and poured her a glass of water.

"Thank you," Ava said and took a gulp from the glass. Water always tasted so good after a night of singing. "You do this every night?"

"Yep."

"That can't be good for you to go on such little sleep."

"Your body gets use it. The Army taught me that."

Ava took another gulp of water.

"Can I tell you something that's been bothering me?" she asked.

"Guess you better now."

"I've been watching you with Ella. You don't show her much affection."

"You've barely been around us together," he replied, leaning back in his chair until it looked as though it would tip backwards.

"I've been around you enough to see it. Everyone can."

"Now you sound like Vivie." His chair hit the floor with a thud, and he leaned forward on his elbows. "I'm trying."

"I don't mean to make you angry, but Ella needs to see that you love her."

"I'm providing for her, aren't I?" he came close to shouting. "The truth is it's still hard for me to even look at her. You don't know what it was like to come home from the war to a dead wife and a daughter you don't even know. Work, classes, Vivie, they all make me forget the pain of it, but one look at her and I'm reliving that pain."

"I'm so sorry," Ava said as tears she knew her brother would hate came rushing down her cheeks. "I shouldn't have said anything."

"As long as you stop crying, it's ok. I'll…I'll…try harder with Ella."

"Thank you," Ava whispered. "Are you excited about the new baby?"

"Estelle wouldn't have wanted Ella to be an only child, and Vivie really wants a baby."

Ava breathed in as her tears began to stop. She now realized that her brother was taking care of her niece as best as he could. Even when it didn't seem like he was thinking about her, he always was. He was right. Estelle would have wanted Ella to have a brother or a sister.

"Oh, I'm sorry about your loss," James said. At first, Ava didn't know what he was talking about, but then a sharp pang gripped her chest as she realized he was talking about her own lost baby. *How does he know?* She couldn't imagine her mother writing to him about it.

"Edwin told me last night while you and Vivie were laying Ella down. He said it's been hard on you."

She looked at him in amazement, unable to believe that Edwin would talk about what happened to them with anyone. She didn't think men talked about serious things.

"Don't be mad at him," he continued when she didn't speak. "It was my fault. I asked him how you were handling his injury, and it just kind of led to that. He's been worried about you, but he said you were doing better, singing again."

"I am," Ava finally spoke. "Since you were honest with me, I'll be honest with you. At first, I wasn't happy about the baby. I was also afraid because of what happened to Estelle and worried about school and the band, but then I did want it, and it was too late."

"I'm sorry for you," James said.

"Let's don't talk about it anymore. I've had enough pep talks and sermons from Mom and Carson."

"I bet you have!" James laughed, and his laughter made her laugh.

The next morning, Vivie woke them up with three quick knocks and an announcement that breakfast was waiting on them. Ava felt as though she had just gotten to sleep. Edwin was already awake and hungry. As soon as they opened the bedroom door, Ella was by her side, and Ava drug herself to the kitchen table. It did smell good, a mixture of bacon and syrup. James was already at the table eating his pecan pancakes and seeming as though he had gotten just as much rest as everyone else. After breakfast, Vivie talked him into playing his banjo for a little while, and then he drove them to meet the band. Ava couldn't wait for her seat on the bus. She was exhausted. Her performance, lack of sleep, and conversation with James had depleted her.

"Good morning," Willie Harold said when they were loading the bus.

"Morning," Ava replied in a daze.

"Hope you had a good night."

"We did," Edwin answered for them.

Ava's heavy legs walked down the aisle of the bus, and she fell onto their usual seat as more band members said hello and asked about their night. It sounded as though they had all had quite the time at the Georgian Terrace. She laid her head against the window and fell asleep. She could rest easy now that she knew Ella was being cared for and her husband wasn't hurting by her side.

Chapter 26

Rosemary followed behind Annamae who continued to rummage through the trays and trays of five and ten cent items at Woolworth's five and dime store.

"Is that all you're buying?" Annamae asked without taking her eyes off an array of sewing needles and thimbles.

"I think so." Rosemary clutched the small hairbrush in her hand. She had been in such a hurry when she left to elope with Percy that she had forgotten many of her personal things. It would be nice not to have to use Percy's too slender of a comb anymore.

"You are a frugal one," Annamae said as she picked up a new thimble and added it to the pile of things she planned to buy.

"Excuse me, mam." A store worker walked past Rosemary with a large woman following behind her. Rosemary moved over to make room for the woman's hips.

"This is where we keep all of our smaller sewing supplies." The employee pointed to the tray Annamae had just left.

Rosemary watched as she assisted the larger woman with her and then began tidying up the rows and rows of sales tables. All of the female staff wore white blouses and matching white skirts. Another worker was on the next row restocking a tray of face cream, and still another was up ahead at the counter taking money from a customer who had finished her shopping. The sight of them all working so busily made her miss Wakefield's. She would much rather be working in a store than shopping in a store.

"Banana split?" Annamae was suddenly behind her.

"Are you finished?"

"Suppose I better be. I don't have your self-control when it comes to money."

They made their way to the lunch counter and ordered sandwiches and ice cream.

Later that afternoon, Rosemary sat in the living room talking with Mrs. Ramsey while she waited for Percy to come home from work.

"Let me know the next time you plan to stop by Woolworth's. There are a few things I am in need of, and the older I get, the more I hate shopping," Mrs. Ramsey said.

"I will," Rosemary replied.

"You should have been at the store back in the late thirties. I'm sure you heard about it all in the news."

"No, not in Alabama. What news?" Rosemary asked.

"That store is where the female workers had their famous sit-down strike. All of them, they say 108, just quit working one afternoon, demanding higher wages, time and a half after 48 hours, free uniforms, and the such. Customers were just left standing there with their money in their hands unable to buy anything. After a few days of that, the store management had to give in. Those girls got everything they asked for."

"That's incredible!" Rosemary said, imagining the incident in her head. "When I worked at a department store in

Anniston, I don't think any of us ever thought of doing such a thing."

"Probably not. Detroit is a progressive city. Those girls got big ideas from working during the war at those factories and from the General Motors strike, which had happened a few days beforehand."

Rosemary smiled thinking of Lorraine Crockett. Her former manager, who was so loyal to Wakefield's, would have never dreamed of leading them in a strike. Still, after being in Detroit, she was proud of those girls she didn't know. She had always thought that she had been paid well, but she was beginning to see the unfairness in the work force.

"Oh, you wanted to know about the young woman in that portrait." Mrs. Ramsey pulled her out of her thoughts and pointed up to the picture of an attractive woman hanging over the book case. The woman had large, brown eyes and a smug start of a smile that seemed to say she knew something you didn't.

"Yes, tell me about her." Rosemary stared up at the portrait.

"That's Rita Ramsey, Thomas's niece. She was a bright one. Exceled at school. Thought she might be the first woman in the family to go the educational way, but one day she went to the circus with some friends and never came back."

"What happened?" Rosemary asked with a horrified look on her face.

"She fell in love with a trapeze artist and became one herself. They toured together for a while and the last we heard of them was that they had settled down in Texas. Oh, Thomas's brother and the rest of the family missed her something awful. They felt as if she had been stolen from them. But I suppose she was happy. She never came home, but Thomas thinks she may show up again one day."

Rosemary swallowed hard. Is that what her parents felt like?

The front door opened, and Percy was home.

"Hi Mrs. Ramsey. Thanks for keeping my wife company." He hugged the older woman as was his custom now.

"Your wife has been the one keeping me company. Sweet, sweet girl. Hang on to her."

"Don't plan on letting her go." Percy grinned at them both.

"Let's go get you cleaned up," Rosemary said. She knew he didn't want to spend the evening talking to Mrs. Ramsey. They told Mrs. Ramsey goodbye and hurried up the stairs as he pretended to almost touch her with his dirty work hands. Manufacturing refrigerator parts had proven to be a messy job.

"If you don't stop, I'll have to wash up before dinner too!" Rosemary laughed.

"We can wash up together!"

"Want me to cook tonight? I have some things in the kitchen I could fix." She ignored his last comment and sat down on their bed as he began to undress.

"Absolutely not!"

"I'm beginning to think you're afraid of my cooking."

"No, but there is no need for you bothering yourself with that when we can just get something out."

She didn't remonstrate. She would go wherever he wanted, which she knew would include an after dinner drink. Every night seemed to.

"Buy anything when you were out shopping with Annamae today?"

"A hairbrush."

"Rosemary, buy yourself some clothes. Enjoy yourself when I'm gone."

"Actually," she began and cleared her throat. "I was thinking today. What if I went back to work at one of the stores?"

He stopped scrubbing his face and turned around and stared at her.

"Why would you want to do that? Don't I provide you with enough?"

"Of course, I just like working. That's all."

"That's nonsense. A girl who doesn't have to work, shouldn't."

She stood up and put her arms around his bare waist.

"You're right. Forget I said anything."

"So you do want to wash up together!" He pulled her closer and laughed.

Chapter 27

Carson gripped the pulpit with both hands as he read from his Grandpa Chester's well-worn King James Bible.

"And it came to pass, that when the Jews which dwelt by them came, they said unto us ten times, 'From all the places whence ye shall return unto us they will be upon you.' Therefore set I in the lower places behind the wall, and on the higher places, I even set the people after their families with their swords, their spears, and their bows. And I looked, and rose up, and said unto the nobles, and to the rulers, and to the rest of the people."

The front door of the church opened, and Carson paused in is reading to look up. For a second, he thought his sister had returned, but the dark-haired woman was followed by an older woman in a fancy hat and not his brother-in-law.

"Be not ye afraid of them: remember the Lord, which is great and terrible, and fight for your brethren, your sons, and your daughters, your wives, and your houses," he continued, trying to place his new arrivals. A second glance told him that they were not anyone he recognized from the church or the community or the neighboring communities.

"God gave Nehemiah a vision," he spoke out to the congregation. More words tumbled out of his mouth as he looked into the woman's face now and realized who she was. *It can't be!* Her eyes were dark like her hair, and her features were delicate, perfectly resembling what he remembered. He looked away and tried to turn his thoughts away from the impossibility of her and back to his sermon, which he hoped was still being delivered in the way he had planned. "This vision was not just for those in Nehemiah's time. It is for us today."

He finished his sermon and the benediction without looking at the woman again and then took his place at the front of the church to speak to each departing person. She and the older woman waited their turn at the back of the line, being greeted by cordial church members on all sides.

"What kind of pound cake did you say it was again?" Carson asked of the cake that had just been placed in his hands. His ears were too intent on hearing what was being asked of the woman to hear much else.

"Lemon," Mrs. Faulkner repeated. "You could stand to gain a few pounds Reverend."

"This will certainly help. Thank you for always thinking of my well-being." He smiled and moved the cake to his left hand so he could shake her husband's hand with his right.

"She feeds you more cake than she does me!" Mr. Faulkner said, and everyone close to them laughed, too loudly for much else to be heard.

Finally, all who were left were the woman, the woman with her, and Mrs. Duncan.

"Maria came all the way from Germany to hear you speak!" Mrs. Duncan exclaimed when he was free.

"Albin's wife?" Carson said, not caring if he stared at her now.

"How do you know?" she asked with a European accent not often heard in Alabama.

"His painting of you," he muttered, blushing at how absurd the idea of recognizing her from a painting must seem.

"My Albin was a good painter."

"Was? Isn't he still?"

"He died," she said gently as a look of accustomed sadness swept over her face, and Carson placed a hand on the pew beside him.

"But how? He was well when he left."

"How did you ever know her husband?" Mrs. Duncan cut in. Carson had forgotten she was still there.

"My husband was a German POW at Fort McClellan. He was in Reverend Stilwell's care for some time," Maria answered for him.

"Well, now doesn't that just beat all?" Mrs. Duncan gasped, and Carson wished she would leave.

"But how could he have died?" he asked again.

"Tuberculosis. He was well when he returned but became very ill six months later."

"I don't know what to say," Carson said, all of his churchy words leaving him. Even though Albin was a German, he had worked alongside him, played checkers with him, watched him paint with his injured hand, and talked life with him. He had been a friend no matter how unlikely.

"So very sorry to hear this news with you, Reverend." Mrs. Duncan patted his back. "I best be getting home. Very nice to make your acquaintances." She nodded at their visitors. "I never thought I would meet anyone from Germany, especially at church."

"Goodbye," Maria and the other woman said as Carson stared down at the cake still in his hands.

"Reverend Stilwell, I should introduce you to my aunt, Bernadette Aubert."

"Please call me Carson. So sorry. Your news is making me forget my manners." Carson extended his hand to the lady by Albin's widow. She was a tall woman in a black, lacy dress with a matching hat that made her pallid skin and light blue eyes stand out.

"Very pleased to meet you." Mrs. Aubert cupped his hand in hers. "Albin spoke so high of you and this place that we had to come see it all and you for ourselves. Some officers at the fort told us where to find you."

"Did you see your husband's artwork?" Carson turned back to Maria.

"No, no one spoke of it."

"Then I will take you myself. Where are you staying?"

"The Bevis Hotel. We have a chauffeur from there picking us up here."

"Can I pick you up at your hotel later this afternoon, say four o'clock?

"Are you sure it wouldn't be too much trouble for you?" she asked, but her bright eyes pleaded otherwise.

"Not at all. Albin would have wanted you to see his paintings."

"Then we accept."

"Cake?" Carson offered, and they laughed.

Carson still knew a few of the remaining officers at Fort McClellan, which seemed to dwindle every day. They liked him and were eager to let him escort Mrs. Sagadin and Mrs. Aubert into Remington Hall, which was the officer's club. The building was as he remembered it. The large, rectangular room through the front entrance still boasted high, dark wooden beams, fireplaces on either side with gold army seals above, and bronze chandeliers. What was missing, however, were the many men he used to see conversing, smoking, and playing cards during their free time.

"Very beautiful," Maria said.

"Certainly," Mrs. Aubert agreed.

"It used to be a rather busy place before the war ended. Now, the fort is just a recruitment training center, and even that is said to be ending soon," Carson explained.

"I hope the fort's purpose is over for good," Maria said, and Carson looked down at her, noticing the sadness he had seen earlier settle over her face again.

"Let's hope so. The murals are through here."

He led them to an adjoining room with an abandoned bar. No one was drinking on a Sunday. Quaint tables were scattered about with a view of lovely Buckner Circle. The view was second, however, to the painted murals running across the top five feet of each wall. Maria immediately found her portrait. She gasped and covered her mouth with her hand as tears began to flow down her face.

"He did love you." Mrs. Aubert put her arms around her niece.

Carson watched them, marveling at the likeness between the woman in the picture and the real woman before him. The only difference was the clothes each was wearing. The woman in the picture wore a blue and white everyday dress with a summer hat. She was sitting and looking into the eyes of a Spanish soldier who appeared to be flirting with her.

"Albin wanted the paintings to be Spanish to match the fort. I don't know if you noticed when we drove through,

151

but most of the buildings here have a Spanish-American design. He also wanted the pictures to tell a soldier's life," Carson told them.

Maria looked away from her painting, and she and Mrs. Aubert began to examine all of the murals throughout the room. There were soldiers in shorts and helmets carrying guns and a dead goose, soldiers in lesser clothes fighting and wrestling, and soldiers in finer clothes participating in everyday village life.

"Albin thought you were the best part of his murals," Carson said. "He made sure that I saw his finished painting of you."

Maria turned toward him and grasped his hand.

"Thank you for being his friend." Her eyes were full of the gratitude she spoke. For Carson too, she was the best part of the murals.

"He may have been a prisoner, but my nephew liked it here," Mrs. Aubert said, and Maria let go of his hand. "He was given good food, a clean place to lay, recreation, and the opportunity to paint. He also thought your country was beautiful."

"What are you doing tomorrow?" Carson asked.

"We have no plans," Mrs. Aubert replied.

"Let me take you on a driving tour of the area. We could visit Weaver Cave."

"We don't want to burden you," Maria said.

"You wouldn't be. I work with my father during the week on our farm. I'll get some things done early and pick you up right after lunch."

"You are kind," Mrs. Aubert said.

"We would love that." Maria smiled and began to circle the room again, admiring her deceased husband's paintings once more.

Chapter 28

Ava scrunched up her eyes and peered into the distance at the front porch. Someone was there. She picked up her pace as the image of her mother sweeping up and down the porch became clearer. Ava sighed. She always felt guilty when her mother did her housework. She paused a minute as the crisp, determined flicks of the broom told her that her mother had not come over to clean. Something was amiss.

"About time," Victoria stopped the broom and greeted her daughter.

"I met Rebekah for lunch. We plan to stay in touch through the summer. What's wrong?"

"Nothing." Victoria stood the broom up by the door and followed her daughter inside. "Do you have any idea what your brother has been up to the last few days?"

"Visiting the hospitals, sermonizing in the barn? I don't know." Ava sat down her purse on the kitchen table and turned to her mother with an unhidden look of amused curiosity now.

"He's been driving German women all over the place."

Ava laughed even though she knew her mother was annoyed.

"What? How does he know any German women?" she asked.

"One is the widow of a German POW your brother befriended, and the other is her aunt."

"How did they find Carson?"

"Through the fort. Anyway," Victoria continued, "he's invited them over to the house Saturday night for dinner, and I want you and Edwin to come over too."

"I don't have a performance that night, so we can come."

"Good," Victoria said and began tidying up her daughter's dish rags, which had been flung across the kitchen counter. "I don't even know what German people like to eat."

"Mom, how could they not like your food?"

"We'll see. I expect you early to help out."

"Yes, mam," Ava replied, not enjoying the thought of Carson and German women as much anymore.

"Germans in this house!" Grandpa Chester kept repeating and shaking his head. "Didn't think I'd live to see the day."

"Well, you did," Victoria said, carrying a big bowl of mashed potatoes to the table. "Would you please wear your shoes tonight, pa? We've never met these people before."

"Alright," he grunted and went to get his boots off the front porch.

"It'll be fun." Sheffield followed his wife with a bowl of peas. "We get to hear things from their side of the story. Edwin, what do you think?"

"I agree, sir," Edwin said from his chair where he was trying to stay out of his mother-in-law's way.

"It just seems so un-American." Victoria placed her hands on her hips and looked over her almost full dinner table.

155

"The war is over, and these two women were not the ones shooting at our son." Sheffield placed a hand on his wife's shoulder.

"Their relatives might have been. Ava, where are those biscuits?"

"Right here." Ava brought an almost overfull basket of bread to the table.

"I'll bring the chicken off the stove when they get here. Don't want it to get cold."

"They're here!" Grandpa Chester hollered as he stepped back into the house with his boots on.

"Goodness me!" Victoria smoothed down the light blue Sunday dress she had chosen to wear for her guests and unpinned the back part of her hair.

"You look beautiful, blossom," Sheffield said, forgetting their approaching guests as he watched his wife's hair fall down past her shoulders in black strands.

"Stop looking at me like that." She couldn't help but smile. "Open the door, Sheffield."

He opened the door, and they all stood by it ready to greet the Germans.

"Welcome, welcome," Sheffield said when Carson and his guests were out of the car and at the steps.

"This is my home." Carson held Mrs. Aubert's arm to steady her as she walked up the stairs.

"Very quaint," she said.

"Mr. Stilwell, I presume," Maria said now to Sheffield. "Thank you for having us in your home."

"Pleased to have you." He escorted them through the door, which Mrs. Aubert had to stoop through for the enormous purple hat she wore. Carson introduced them all quickly to the rest of the family.

"Let's do sit down and eat together." Victoria pointed toward the table and then dashed into the kitchen for the chicken.

"I haven't seen this much food since before the war," Mrs. Aubert remarked.

"Glad to have you at our table," Sheffield said.

"We didn't know what people in Germany ate," Grandpa Chester remarked, and Victoria frowned at him as she set down a platter piled high with fried chicken in the center of the table.

"This looks wonderful," Maria said and laughed. "We like many things."

Sheffield prayed, and everyone helped themselves to the food.

"How do you like Alabama?" Ava asked.

"It's beautiful, and the people are friendly," Mrs. Aubert answered.

"Just as Albin said," Maria added.

"You speak good English," Grandpa Chester said and bit into the chicken leg he was holding.

"That is because of my aunt," Maria replied. "She is from Great Britain."

"Is that so?" Victoria smiled and passed Mrs. Aubert, or an American ally as she would tell the garden club, the basket of biscuits.

"Yes, I moved to Germany as a girl and married Maria's uncle when I was a very young woman."

"Did your husband not want to come with you to America?" Sheffield asked.

"My husband is no longer living," Mrs. Aubert answered.

"I'm sorry to hear that."

"Except for Maria's younger brother, I'm afraid all of the men in our family are now deceased. My husband died of a heart attack before the war started, Albin's brother Ernst died in the war, and Albin died of tuberculosis after the war. We also lost Maria's father when the Russians invaded Berlin."

Everyone stopped eating and fell silent for a moment.

"We know many who lost family members to the war, but our homes were never invaded," Carson said.

"How dreadful and to lose so many in your family." Victoria's eyes watered as she looked at her guests across the table.

"We are learning to live on," Mrs. Aubert said. "Berlin was in utter shambles but is being rebuilt every day. The women have seen to that." Her hat shook with her last words.

"I'm sure your women endured much," Victoria empathized. "Even here, women had to work men's jobs and manage households alone."

"Edwin, Carson said you were in Europe during the war. Did you ever come to Germany?" Mrs. Aubert asked.

"No, I was mostly in Italy," Edwin replied.

"Our son James saw a little of Germany," Sheffield said.

"Too bad we can't meet him and get his opinion of our country. I consider myself a German woman first and a British woman second as I have lived most of my life there."

"How long will be you here?" Ava asked before helping herself to another spoonful of mashed potatoes. They were creamier tonight than usual. Her mother always cooked better for company.

"Another week or two. We have nothing to go back to and are in no hurry."

"I'm taking them to see the Anniston Rams play at Johnston Field on Saturday," Caron announced and smiled at Maria who had fallen silent beside him when they began talking about Berlin and her family.

"Yes, we are looking forward to watching American baseball!" Maria's eyes brightened again, and she smiled back at him.

"Should be a good game," Sheffield said. "The Rams won the league title last year."

"You should all join us for the game." Maria smiled at them all now.

"My garden club will be meeting," Victoria said. "Ava, you and Edwin should go with them."

"I can't. I'll be with the band in Nashville, remember?" Ava replied.

"Oh, I forgot you two would be gone."

"The band is leaving Friday, so Edwin can't go."

"Edwin's not going!" Victoria looked at her daughter with scolding eyes. "Do you mean to tell me that you will be traveling alone as the only female with that band."

"Mom, I'll be safe. They take good care of me, and Edwin doesn't mind."

"She'll be fine. It won't be long," Edwin said to help his wife but avoided his mother-in-law's gaze.

"Have you been shopping in Anniston?" Ava asked Maria and Mrs. Aubert to remind her mother of their guests.

It worked. The conversation turned to the many shops of Anniston and away from her weekend plans for the rest of the dinner. They sat and talked over coffee and then made ready to leave. Carson was driving them back to Anniston.

"That is the biggest hat I've ever seen," Grandpa Chester said to Mrs. Aubert when it was his turn to tell their guests goodnight, and Victoria coughed behind him.

"A woman with a good hat never loses her pride. Goodnight to you all and thank you again," Mrs. Aubert replied and left with her niece.

Sheffield closed the door behind them, and Victoria sighed. She had successfully entertained two German women despite her father. She would have much to tell the garden club on Saturday.

Chapter 29

The band's performance in Atlanta at the Georgian Terrace Hotel gained them an even farther booking in Nashville, TN. Ava sat up straight on her stool next to the band, listening as they played Begin the Beguine and watching the many dancing couples twirl, bounce, and sway with the song the Harry James Orchestra had made popular. If Edwin was there, she too would be dancing, but no dancing for her tonight, just singing when she was needed and enjoying the many sounds of the saxophone, trumpet, bass, and drums. Their trumpet player, Jonathan, was magnificent tonight. Maybe not as good and bombastic as Harry James, but his playing was light, fluid, and pleasing to the ear. She drummed her foot to the beat and looked up at the American flags and banners hanging above them. It was Friday night, July 4, 1947, and the patriotic party was in full swing. She wore a blue dress with red ribbons in her hair, red high heels, and her usual red lipstick for the occasion. She closed her eyes now and let the music, which was her life, fill her.

Later that night, she lay in bed missing the other part of her life. Being in a hotel over two hundred miles from home just wasn't as much fun without Edwin. She stretched out her arms and legs and felt the softness of the sheets. The band chose to stay in a less expensive hotel across from the hotel where they were playing, but it was still nice.

There was a loud banging noise in the hallway outside her room and then even louder voices. A couple was arguing. She lay very still listening. "You…, don't…., that woman…, told….," she could only make out some words of the noisy conversation. They were moving further down the hall, and she was glad of it. She closed her eyes, and soon the tiredness she always felt after a performance put her to sleep. More loud noises woke her a few hours later. Men were laughing and hollering as they passed her room. She heard her door knob turn and then someone shake it.

"Wrong room," a man said, and more laughing followed.

She exhaled and pushed her body down deeper under her covers, hoping their next concert was at a time when Edwin could be with her.

Chapter 30

Except for the heat, it was the perfect day for baseball. The sky was a brilliant blue, and there was a light breeze that sporadically blew relief into the crowd's faces.

"My apologies that my aunt could not come with us," Maria said again from her seat in the stands beside Carson. "She cannot tolerate very warm weather."

"I understand. I'm glad you could still come," he replied, hoping the last part of his remark didn't sound too forthright.

"Me too." She shielded her eyes from the sun and smiled up at him much as the girl in the painting smiled up at the Spanish soldier. He thought again about how much prettier she was in real life than in the painting and quickly turned his eyes to the field where the Anniston Rams and Montgomery Rebels were warming up on opposite sides of the outfield.

"Do you watch baseball in Germany?" he asked.

"No. It is not a popular sport in my country. My brother Berty plays hand ball."

"I've never heard of hand ball." Carson watched the Ram's starting pitcher, Wes Flowers, wind up for a practice pitch.

"It is as it sounds. You throw balls into a goal."

He laughed at her simple answer.

"Did Berty fight in the war?"

163

At this question, Maria laughed, and Carson looked back into her face. He was used to her somber seriousness when the war was mentioned, but her brown eyes glowed now instead.

"Hitler may have taken many things, but my mother was not letting him have our Berty. He was only five when the war began, but as it dragged on and younger and younger boys started fighting, my mother worried more and more. She and Berty left Berlin and went to live with my oma, or grandmother as Americans would say, for a while. She was determined to hide him as best as she could."

"I'm glad of it." Carson smiled down at her. "I don't know if I told you, but my mother was ecstatic when I was classified 4-F on account of my eyesight and couldn't fight in the war. I blame her prayers for my bad eyes."

Maria's eyes sparked again as she laughed, and Carson's face grew as hot as the day thinking of how nice it was to laugh with her.

"Mothers are a powerful force. I'm glad you did not fight."

Carson didn't have to reply. The crowd stood to their feet and cheered as the Rams took the field and the ballgame began. It was an intense, close game that took the Rams a long nine innings to win. Carson was afraid that Maria would tire of the game, but she never did. She asked question after question about it, and he answered them all as they ate peanuts and watched together.

"I would like to play baseball," Maria said when the game ended and they were walking back to his car.

"I could teach you. My brother James and I used to play all the time."

"What about tomorrow?"

Carson laughed. He didn't think she would take his offer serious.

"If you want to play, I could pick you up tomorrow afternoon after church. Would your aunt like to learn too?" They were now at the car, and Carson opened her door for her.

"Certainly not! She would rather die than play ball in the heat." She waved her hand at the absurdity of her aunt playing baseball and got into the car. "I'll have to go without her again."

"Just you and me then." Carson closed the door behind her, wishing he hadn't said that last part. *Will it be a date or just more Alabama hospitality?*

When Carson arrived at the Bevis Hotel the following afternoon, Maria was already waiting for him in the hotel lobby. She wore navy pants and a light blue blouse, and her hair was tied back in a matching scarf. Carson hadn't seen a woman in pants since Vivie, and he smiled to himself as he remembered the commotion the pants had caused at Christmas. It was a good thing he wasn't taking her to his mother's for dinner again.

"Are you laughing at me?" Maria asked.

"No, I would never do that," he said quickly and wiped the smile from his face. "I was just thinking about how I never thought I would play baseball with any girl besides my sister. Most girls aren't interested in it."

"I am excited to learn an American sport. I can tell everyone at home that I played baseball! Berty will be very pleased."

"Let's go then," Carson said and led her out the door.

He drove them to an old ballfield in Jacksonville that he played on all his life. A group of kids were in the middle of a game, so he took her to the grassy area next the field and handed her a glove.

"Wear this on your left hand. It's mine, so I'm afraid it will be big for you."

She placed the glove on her hand and squeezed it together with her fingers.

"I feel like a player already," she said, and he smiled at the determination on her face.

He placed James's glove on his left hand and ran a short distance from her.

"We'll start with some warm-up throws." He grasped the small, grass and mud-stained ball in his hand.

"Ready?" he yelled.

"Ready!" she yelled back.

He threw the ball gently toward her. The ball brushed the tip of her glove and fell behind her. She ran to pick it up and then threw it back to him much harder than expected.

"Whew," he said, feeling a slight sting on his left hand. "You can throw!"

"What did you expect," she replied, and they laughed as he threw it again. She barely missed a second time but threw it back just as hard.

"Follow the ball with your eyes all the way to the glove," Carson repeated what he had heard his father say many times when he was a boy. She nodded as he threw the ball again. This time she caught it, and she jumped up and down with the ball in her glove.

"That's it!" Carson shouted, loving the way her eyes danced and her nose crinkled up when she was happy.

When she caught several more, he stepped back farther away from her for longer throws. He had forgotten how much fun it was to play catch.

"Do you want to try batting now?" he asked when the kids had finished their game and were racing each other off the field.

"Yes!" she answered.

They moved to the field, and he stood behind home plate and demonstrated holding the bat and swinging.

"I think I can do that." Maria took the bat from him and stood by home plate. She gripped it at its handle and bent over the plate.

"Choke up on the bat. It will help your swing," Carson said as he backed away from her with the ball.

"What?" She looked down at the bat in her hands.

"Move your hands up the bat."

"Like this?" She moved her hands up an inch or so above the end of the bat.

"More." He jogged to her and repositioned her hands midway up the bat handle, right over left. Her skin was soft, and he avoided her eyes as he let go and ran back to the pitcher's mound.

"Just like catching, follow the ball with your eyes all the way to the bat."

"Yes, coach!" she said and laughed. She gripped the bat with all her strength and watched as Carson wound up his pitch. He stopped, hesitated, and wound up again, hoping the pitch would make it over the plate and not directly at her. It was a soft pitch but it did make it to the plate. Maria swung as hard as she could and made contact. It was a shallow pop fly, and Carson easily caught it.

"I did it!" Maria jumped up and down.

"You did!" Carson ignored the urge to run and grab her hands and jump with her. "Want another?" he asked instead.

"Yes, please." She was already back at the plate, bat in hand, and peering up at him eagerly. He pitched again. This time it dribbled toward third base.

"Run to first base!" he yelled, lunging for the ball and pretending to bobble it as she ran to the base. He made for the base, stopped, and stood laughing when he saw she was there, hands on her hips, grinning at him.

"German women can play baseball!" She laughed with him.

They played awhile longer and then started back to Anniston.

"I had a good time. Thank you for teaching me baseball," she said.

"Hope you got some good pitches. James was always the pitcher. I played shortstop."

"You were perfect," she said, and Carson blushed. "This day was perfect. It made me forget for a little while all that's happened, the war, Albin, my father."

Carson gripped the steering wheel harder to keep from taking her hand.

"God often grants us moments of peace and joy even in the midst of pain. As the psalmist says 'the Lord is close to the brokenhearted,'" he said, his Bible and the pulpit never far away. He hoped she liked that part of him, the most important part.

"At times, the war made me think there wasn't God. Many horrible things happened in Berlin." She shuddered. "Being here makes me think differently. I want to come hear you speak at your church again before we leave next week."

"You're leaving next week?" Carson asked and swallowed hard.

"Yes, it will have been almost four weeks, and my aunt is getting anxious to be home."

"Are you?" He could feel the stupidity of his question burning on his face.

"No, there are too many painful memories back in Berlin, but I must."

He glanced at her face. She was looking out her window to something other than the house they were driving past.

"You could always come back," he suggested.

She laughed and looked at him now.

"Maybe, I will. I like baseball!"

Chapter 31

Rosemary clutched her shopping bag as she walked up the steps to the Ramseys' front door. She couldn't wait to show Percy what she had bought him and the other surprise hiding at the bottom of the bag in the palm of her hand. If she hurried she would have just enough time to bathe and redress before he got home from work. She wiped perspiration from the warm day off her forehead and couldn't resist pausing at the top step to admire the trees beside the house. They were the greenest she had seen them yet, and she could hear squirrels playing in their uppermost branches. She pulled out her house key from her dress pocket and unlocked the door.

"Hello, sweetheart," Mrs. Ramsey called out from where she sat crocheting on the couch.

"Hello, Mrs. Ramsey," Rosemary replied, making herself pause in the doorway. "Hope your day has been good."

"Very nice, dear." Mrs. Ramsey peered up at her through her reading glasses. "Your husband is already home."

Rosemary's whole body stiffened with the news. He being home early could only mean more work setbacks.

"Good! I'll go up and see him." She managed a smile and then collected herself as she climbed the steps. Everything was quiet and undisturbed as if he wasn't home, but she knew Mrs. Ramsey wouldn't tease her. She opened the door to their room and saw him sitting at the small desk in the corner. He was lounged back in the chair, shirtless. His hair was a mess, and a large liquor bottle sat in front of him half empty. His haughty eyes turned slowly upon her as she closed the door.

"Where have you been?" he asked, looking at her face, hair, dress, and the bag in her hands.

"Shopping with Annamae. I got you some new shirts." She tried to smile but failed. It was the first time that she knew of that he had brought liquor into their home. He drank every evening when they were out but not at home, not in the room they shared.

"Now you buy something, now when I'm temporarily laid off!" He laughed at her and turned his eyes back to the table and the bottle. She watched as he poured himself another drink.

"Are you drunk?"

"Of course, I'm drunk," he shouted back, and she hoped Mrs. Ramsey didn't hear or know what state he was in. "I'm not the saint your Navy boy was. Maybe, you should have married him."

Tears began to sting Rosemary's eyes, but she wouldn't cry yet. She quietly reopened the door and left him, still mindful of Mrs. Ramsey. She heard him laugh again as the door shut. She made it to the next room and dropped to her knees as tears now began to course down her face and fall onto her hands and arms.

That's the alcohol talking, not your uncle, she heard her mother speak in her mind. She had often been told that as a child about her uncle Lewis, the one she hadn't seen in years and no one spoke of anymore.

"Lord, help…Percy….help….me," she said in between gasps. *He has to still love me, especially now. It was just the*

171

alcohol, not him. The last part of her thoughts she kept repeating to herself over and over again as she sank to the floor and pulled her knees up to her chest. He had horribly betrayed her once, but he had never said anything unkind to her before. *It has to be that awful liquor. Why does he think he needs it?*

For a long time, she listened for him next door, but she heard nothing except the sound of his chair scooting backward and forward. She cried some more when she realized he wasn't coming for her. Her stomach growled, but she had no desire to eat. Somehow, she finally fell asleep, too tired to even dream. She awoke early the next morning when the sun began to pour through the unshielded window. She squinted her eyes and looked up at it, remembering what had happened and why she was on the floor. She got up and listened at the door – nothing but the faint sound of the Ramseys' radio from downstairs. She tiptoed out and opened their bedroom door. Percy was sprawled out on top of the bed covers as though he had gone to sleep where he had fallen. He didn't hear her. He didn't move. She stood watching him a moment and then quietly gathered a change of clothes. She went back to their other room, dressed, combed her hair, and found the bag of things she had been so proud of the day before. She hid the smallest item in her purse and then left. Luckily, Mr. and Mrs. Ramsey were occupied and not near the door. Once outside, she gulped down the morning air as new tears began to emerge.

I will not cry anymore. I will do what has to be done. She eased her pace, knowing the stores weren't open yet. She walked circles through the streets of Detroit, waiting. Finally, they were open. She returned the shirts she had bought Percy

172

and then made her way to Woolworth's. The store was already busy despite the early hour.

"Good morning," one of the shop girls greeted her.

"Good morning," Rosemary replied. "I'd like to apply for a job."

The girl, who was wearing more make-up than Rosemary thought necessary, smiled and looked her over.

"You'll have to see our store manager. Follow me."

Rosemary followed and met with the manager, who had little time for her but appreciated her past experience. With a white uniform of her own now, she left and made her way back home. Her thoughts turned again to her husband. *What will he say?*

Back at the house, Rosemary hurried through the door and back up the steps, thankful that the Ramseys were still out of sight. This time when she opened the bedroom door, Percy was up, dressed, and pacing the floor. He ran to her and gripped both of her arms.

"I'm so sorry," he said. "I wasn't myself last night. I thought you had left me."

She let him hug her, but she wasn't ready to embrace him herself yet.

"What's this?" he asked feeling the bag between them.

"My uniform," she answered. "I'm starting a job at Woolworth's on Monday."

Percy let her go, his face reddening.

"I told you I don't want you working."

"I know, but I want to help out. I can bring in money while you're out of work."

He glared at her and then kicked the waste basket by the door.

"No wife of mine is working. Take back that uniform, and I don't ever want to hear another word about it."

She shook with tears at his demand, and he softened, taking her in his arms again.

"You don't have to work. I'll take care of you. I promise."

"Forgive me," she whispered and embraced him back. "I knew how you felt. I just wanted to help."

"I know," he said in her ear and ran his fingers through her hair. "I'll be back to work soon, and you won't ever have to worry about anything."

His shirt was now damp from her tears. She saw the empty bottle from the night before over his shoulder and breathed in, hoping his words were true.

Chapter 32

Mrs. Duncan, Mrs. Faulkner, Mrs. Webb, and Mrs. Ragsdale stood huddled together waving and smiling as Carson drove away from the church with Maria and Mrs. Aubert. He looked back at them through the rearview mirror, knowing that he and his returning female visitors would be the topic of much discussion this afternoon.

"So happy we got to hear you speak once more," Mrs. Aubert said from the back seat. "How do you pick your sermon topics each week?"

"Holy Spirit," he answered. "God prompts my heart toward something each week. It also helps to know your congregation's needs." He glanced at Maria, hoping she enjoyed his message as well, but he couldn't see her face. She was staring out the window again as if her mind were miles and miles away from the car and him.

"What kind of cake is this?" Mrs. Aubert asked of the cake sitting beside her.

"Chocolate pound cake, I believe," Carson said.

"I've never seen women who like to bake cakes so much!"

He laughed, and Maria straightened up in her seat.

"If Albin had to be a prisoner, I'm glad it was here. He was treated kindly. I feel his presence here." She smiled a melancholy smile, and again, Carson longed to reach out for her hand and comfort her.

"His life was too short but good," Mrs. Aubert remarked. "Now, we can go home knowing that."

Carson felt his stomach flip with the words. He drove them back to Anniston, and they ate Sunday lunch at the Sanitary Café. The turkey and dressing was good but not as good as his mother's. She always made it with her fresh biscuits and corn bread.

"I will miss your food," Mrs. Aubert said after another bite of green beans and bacon.

"I expected Albin to come back from the war too skinny, but he wasn't." Maria smiled and tried a forkful of mashed potatoes.

"If you ask me, they fed him here a little too well." Mrs. Aubert laughed. "He weighed more after the war than before the war!"

They all laughed now.

"Did he ever play checkers with you after he got home?" Carson asked.

"Checkers?" Maria looked confused and then smiled. "I do remember him mentioning that you beat him often at some game."

"We played it several times during rainstorms."

"I wish we would have played it then."

Carson started to ask if she wanted to play it the next day but then remembered they were leaving in the morning. He didn't want the afternoon to end. They finished their lunch and then headed back to the Bevis Hotel. He stood with them in the lobby, reluctant to leave.

"Thank you for taking care of an old lady and a widow these last few weeks," Mrs. Aubert said and kissed Carson on the cheek.

"It was a pleasure," Carson replied.

"I have much packing to do. Goodbye, dear boy."

"I'll be up in a bit," Maria said to her aunt, and Carson's heart leapt. Maybe, she was reluctant to leave him too.

They watched Mrs. Aubert leave them, her tall olive hat bobbing up and down as she walked, and then Maria smiled up at him.

"Albin talked about you and this place so much that I had to see for myself. You didn't disappoint."

"I hope not." Carson smiled back down at her as color rose up in his cheeks. "If you come back, I'll play checkers with you next time."

Maria laughed, stood up on her toes, and kissed him on the cheek as her aunt had done. Carson's whole body grew warm from her touch, and he grabbed her hand.

"Can I write to you?"

"Of course," she replied, not removing her hand. "I'll try to write something interesting back."

"You can write to me about anything. I'll find it interesting."

She looked away at this last declaration, and he let go of her hand.

"Let me write down my address for you." She found a pen and a paper receipt from Wakefield's Department Store in her purse and wrote down her address on the back of it.

"I expect to hear from you soon," she said when she was finished and gave him the address.

"You will," he promised.

"Goodbye, then." She held out her hand, and he took it once more.

"Goodbye." They stood looking at each other for a moment, and then she abruptly hugged him, turned, and walked away.

He walked out of the hotel both elated by her touch and depressed by her leaving. For a moment, he stood, not knowing what to do next. Once again, his life was unclear. He walked back to the car and drove home. He needed the barn, a place to pray about the many things he was feeling.

Chapter 33

Ava loved the freer days of summer. No classes meant more time to read and practice her music. She walked slowly to the mailbox, book in hand. The Tolstoy novel was too good to put down. Her mother would be horrified that she read all day and didn't do one bit of housework. She finished the page she was on, reached inside the mailbox, and immediately saw Rosemary's handwriting. She closed her book and ran back to the house with the letter. She hadn't heard from her cousin in two weeks, and she couldn't wait to hear what Rosemary thought about Carson and his German women. Now at the porch, she put the book she hadn't been able to part with all day aside and sat down on the top step. Her fingers started to break open the letter's seal, but the heat of the day stopped her. No one was around; so, she pulled off her sandals and pulled up the yellow skirt of her dress above her knees. Comfortable, she opened the letter and read.

Dear Ava,

I am sorry I haven't written in a week or so. Things have been difficult here. I wish you were here in person to talk to, but this letter will have to do. Please don't tell anyone what I am about to tell you. I have to pour out my feelings somehow. I shouldn't have been so hard on you about telling Edwin you were expecting. I didn't understand how you could keep something of that importance to yourself. It seemed selfish, but now I understand. Ava, I'm pregnant. I found out a few weeks ago, but I can't tell Percy yet. He's out of work again. Bundy has issued temporary layoffs while they prepare for a new contract. Percy was told that it wouldn't be for long, but he still hasn't been called back yet. He's drinking a lot, and I'm scared. We barely had enough money to pay our rent this month. I don't know what will happen next month if he isn't called back. I wanted to get a job at another store, but he wouldn't hear of it. He really wouldn't want me to work if he knew I was pregnant. I just can't tell him yet. It would put even more stress on him and might cause him to drink even more. Pray that he will be called back soon. Pray that he will let me help him. I want to so badly. I'm also sad. I always imagined that expecting a baby would be a time of shared joy, but it's not. I don't want to bring a baby into a world of sadness. So sorry, Ava. I hope me having a baby doesn't make you sad with what happened to you. How are you? How is everyone back at home? Have the German women left yet? I wished I could have been at that dinner table too. Do you really think Carson is smitten with her? Well, I guess I've rambled on enough. Percy is sleeping, and I want to get this letter out to mail before he wakes up. Write soon!

  Love,
  Rosemary

  Ava let the letter fall in her lap and lay back on the familiar, wooden porch. The board just above the top step was slightly bent in, and she could feel the dent with the small of her back. *Why does everyone have to have babies?* She knew it was selfish, but she was tired of all the babies. Sure, every time she thought of the child she miscarried, she felt a pang of sorrow, but even then, she really wasn't ready for her life to change. She hadn't been ready to care for another person more than herself and Edwin, but she had accepted it and grown happy about it until... A wasp flew over her head, and her gray eyes watched it circle around looking for a new place to build a nest. If it did, Edwin would have another one to take down. *Why do they like our porch so much?* She sighed and vowed to pray forgiveness later for her selfishness. It hadn't been a good year. She had lost a baby, Edwin had been injured, and Rosemary had left her. A baby made Rosemary seem even farther away from her than Detroit. Whatever people liked to say, children changed things. Floraline never had time for anything else anymore. The wasp flew off, and she sat up, reclining on her hands. She looked down at her bare feet and red toenails.

"I hate him," she spoke out loud. "Lord, forgive me for hating someone." As much as she knew it was wrong, though, she hated Percy Bledsoe. He stole her cousin from them all and was now making her life miserable. *If he would have never come back here...If he would have been killed in...,* she stopped that train of thought, which was too awful to even think. If it wasn't for "that man," as her mother would say, Rosemary would still be here, working at the store, probably engaged to Jake while he finished medical school, and not having a baby! She heard a whistle and looked up. Edwin was walking down the driveway to their house. She jumped up, the letter falling off her lap and to the ground, and ran to him.

Thank you for bringing him back, she prayed of her own husband and threw her arms around him. The pain from his burns had finally subsided, and she could hug him freely again.

181

"Wow!" He laughed as he dropped his lunch pail with her embrace. "I wish you were this happy to see me every day."

"I am," she said and kissed him.

Ava and Rosemary prayed from different ends of the country over the next week, and to Rosemary's great relief, Bundy called Percy back to work. Now, she just prayed that another temporary layoff was not in their future. They were out celebrating with a group of Percy's work buddies, which included Johnny and Annamae. The men laughed and joked as if the last month hadn't been a hardship, and Rosemary tried to be as relaxed as they all were.

"You haven't heard the best news," Percy said loudly over his friends.

"And what's that?" asked a man named Ralph who Rosemary had just met.

Percy climbed up in his chair with his drink in hand, and Rosemary's whole body tensed.

"My wife is having a baby!" he announced. Everyone at their table and all the tables surrounding them clapped. Rosemary tried to smile as a rush of "Congratulations" came at her from all sides.

"Guess you were busy during the layoff!" Ralph laughed, and all the men and some of the women laughed with him.

"You have to make the most of every situation." Percy put an arm around her, and she was glad that he was happy about it at least. He had actually been ecstatic when she placed the ivory baby shoes in his hands the night before. He kissed her cheek. His lips were warm from the alcohol. It was the first time she had seen him drink all week, but it was in fun and not out of misplaced need this time.

"I can't believe you didn't tell me," Annamae said from her other side, her blue eyes round with surprise.

"We were waiting for the right time."

"I couldn't keep something like that to myself at all!"

"It wasn't easy," Rosemary replied, thinking of how hard it truly had been to keep from her own husband.

"I know nothing about babies. Are you scared?"

"No, I helped out with my sister a lot when she was little."

"That's good. I'd be terrified. Guess I'll learn one day, though. I would like to have a baby before Nan. Her old butcher of a husband might be too old to father children anyways."

Rosemary just smiled at her friend. She never knew what to say when Annamae talked about her convoluted family. She was always taught that you never speak ill of a person's family even if they do.

They finished their late dinner and left for home.

"That was fun," Percy said, entwining his fingers through hers and leading her through the busy sidewalks. He looked back at her and smiled.

"Rosemary, you'll be the best mother there ever was." She could hear the tenderness in his voice even with all the noise around them.

"I love you," he spoke again, and she squeezed his hand. That much, she never doubted.

Chapter 34

"Ava! Ava!" Ava heard her name being called and looked out the open window. The second she saw her mother leaping across the yard she knew that the year of babies continued.

"Ava! Ava!" Victoria kept hollering as she climbed the stairs and opened their unlocked front door. Ava quickly closed the book she had been reading and jumped up as if her mother had caught her in the middle of something.

"I can't keep it to myself until your dad and brother get in from the fields," Victoria said and clutched her sides, which were aching from her dash between their houses. Black strands of hair had come loose from her bun and were scattered across her face. "The baby was born earlier than expected, this past Tuesday, August 19th!"

"Boy or girl?"

"Another girl!" Victoria bounced up and down with her words. "Ella has a sister, and I have a new granddaughter!"

Ava smiled at her mother's enthusiasm, and Victoria grabbed her daughter's hands.

"You're not upset by this news are you? I know your baby would have been here around the same time."

"No, of course not." Ava pulled her hands away and frowned. "And I wish everyone would quit asking me that."

"Who's everyone?" Victoria narrowed her eyes and looked keenly into her daughter's face.

"No one, I just see it on everyone's face when Vivie's baby is mentioned." That was true, but she had been thinking about Rosemary. "And what's my new niece's name?" Ava asked, relieved to see her mother's attention shift back to the baby.

"Jacqueline Elaine Stilwell," her mother announced as if she were reading it from the garden club roll. "You and Edwin come over tonight. We have to celebrate. I'm going to go home and make a cake right now."

She hurried out the door before Ava could even agree to come and somehow managed to make a cake and a better than usual dinner in the few hours before they were all together around the table.

"Jacqueline," Grandpa Chester said as he started on his second piece of chocolate iced cake. "Never heard of it. Sounds too much like Jack. Why can't people name their kids normal names anymore? What's wrong with Jane or Anne or Annie for that matter?" he asked and winked at Ava.

"Oh, pa!" Victoria said. "I think Jacqueline is a very pretty name. It has an elegant ring to it."

"There you go talking like your own mother!"

"I think it sounds like a name from a book," Ava said before putting the bite of cake with the most icing in her mouth. She always saved the best part for last.

"And that's dangerous." Grandpa Chester shook his fork at them. "Those characters in those books are always getting into trouble.

Carson and Ava grinned at each other across the table.

"Please don't do to this poor child what you did to Ava. Call her by her rightful name even if you don't like it." Victoria shook her fork back at him.

"You like being called Annie, don't ya?" Grandpa Chester looked over at his granddaughter.

"I like you calling me Annie," Ava answered without meeting her mother's eyes.

"All I want to know is when do I get to see this new baby girl?" Sheffield asked.

"I've been considering it," Victoria replied. "Why not next weekend? By then, she may feel like house guests and her mother may need to get back to her own duties. I know they will still need help with Ella too."

"Perfect!" Sheffield clapped a hand on the table, and all the plates shook a little. "I'll ask Jude to lead music at the church. Ava, will you play the piano for your mother?"

Ava's gulp of milk stuck in her throat a moment.

"Me? I mean, I can, but I'm not as practiced as Mom."

"You'll do fine. Carson can you manage the animals without me?"

"Yep," he replied.

"I can help out too, sir," Edwin said as he helped himself to another slice of cake.

"Perfect!" Sheffield smiled at them all. "It's settled then. We meet our new granddaughter next weekend!"

Ava's back ached from sitting so straight on the piano stool.

"Standing, standing, standing on the promises of God my Savior," the congregation sang in unison.

Just then, Ava hit a wrong piano key. Jude's good eye immediately turned upon her, but his glass one stay focused forward. She gave him a sheepish smile and studied the notes harder.

"Second verse," he called out, both eyes back on his choir of church goers.

"Standing on the promises that cannot fail. When the howling storms of doubt and fear assail, by the living Word of God I shall prevail, standing on the promises of God," the congregation continued to sing, oblivious to her bad note.

Ava's fingers awkwardly maneuvered the piano keys that her mother's fingers flew over every other Sunday morning. She would practice the piano more, and she would stop being as critical of the band when a new musical piece didn't sound as it should at first. The song ended, and Ava gladly left the piano to take her usual place next to Edwin on the fourth row of the left side. Myrtle's eyes caught hers as she passed the front row with a funny sort of expression, and Ava knew right away that Rosemary must have written to her mother about her pregnancy.

Brother Penny preached about Daniel and the Lion's Den, Ava took her place again at the piano, and the church service ended with another hymn. Judith was out of her seat the moment the last note rang out, racing to play outside in the dirt with all the other children who were tired of sitting still.

"Did Rosemary write to you too?" Myrtle met Ava at the piano and whispered.

"She did," Ava said, hoping Myrtle wouldn't ask her how long she had known.

"What do you think?"

"It's great," Ava replied as innocently as possible.

"I don't know." Myrtle clasped her fidgety hands together and suppressed a nervous giggle. "Babies are wonderful, but she's so far away. Who will help her with everything?"

"Percy, I suppose." At this, Myrtle gave the floor a hard stare.

"Something isn't right with him," she said, and Ava wondered just what Rosemary had confided in her mother.

"Just a mother's feeling, though, that's all," Myrtle continued when Ava didn't respond. "Of course, all she could really talk about in her letter was how she hoped her having a baby didn't bother you."

"I'm fine," Ava said quickly, frustration renewing within her. If she heard the word "baby" one more time, she might explode but not for the reasons they all thought.

"It will happen for you again one day." Myrtle smiled, and Ava's insides grimaced as she tried to smile back.

"Thanks." Ava stepped down from the stage, and Myrtle did too. She felt like racing out of the church like Judith.

"Good piano playing today," Alice Fitzpatrick called out from her circle of fellow garden club members. Unruly children rather than flowers seemed to be the topic of the day.

"Thank you," Ava said back. She was beside Edwin now. She pinched the back of his arm, and he turned toward her, understanding her meaning.

"Picnic by the creek?" she asked once they had said their hurried goodbyes to everyone and shook Brother Penny's hand.

"Sounds like a plan." Edwin smiled down at her, and she sighed happily, knowing that he at least wouldn't want to talk about babies, babies, and babies.

Chapter 35

It was September again, and Ava went gladly back to school for the second half of her third year at Jacksonville State Teacher's College. It felt good to be back in the familiar hallways and classrooms, and she had all the distraction she wanted from family baby talk. The campus was the liveliest she had ever seen it. Registration had exceeded 1,000, and new faces could be seen in every direction. There was also a lot of buzz about the French Ambassador and his wife visiting the school in October.

"In honor of Ambassador Henri Bonnet and his wife Madame Bonnet visiting our college, we are going to perform our school alma mater in French for them during their visit," Mrs. Wheeler announced to her choral group of girls. Some cheered, and others looked bewildered at the thought of singing in a foreign language.

"I know you are all wondering how we can do that. I'm certainly not well versed in the French language, but some members of the French Club have agreed to join us for rehearsal and help us learn how to pronounce the lyrics properly."

Ava smiled at her friend Rebekah and pressed her hands together. She had always thought that singing in another language would be romantic and exciting even if it was for a political figure.

"But for today, let's warm up. I hope you have all been working out those vocal chords during the summer months." Mrs. Wheeler took her seat at the piano and played up the musical scale as they all "Mmmmed" each note.

Ava finished her chorus class, music theory class, individual voice lesson class, and her less than enjoyable math class. She didn't understand why Fine Arts majors were required to know anything about mathematics! The school's electric organ played and was amplified over the campus as the afternoon dwindled, and Ava walked down the steps of Bibb Graves Hall.

"Ice cream?" Rebekah asked when she and another girl named Suzanne caught up with her.

"You bet!" Ava said, knowing she would still have time to beat Edwin back home.

Instead of ice cream, Ava spent the next late afternoon pounding out musical notes on her mother's piano and committing them to memory for her music theory class.

"Light fingers," Victoria called out from the kitchen where she was already cutting up chicken.

"Not performing, Mom, just listening," Ava called back.

"All the same, light fingers make for a clearer sound to listen to."

"Yes, mam," Ava said. If she just agreed, maybe her mother would quit interrupting her studies.

She played and listened, jotted down some notes, and played and listened some more. Willie Harold always complimented her on her musical ear, but nevertheless, the class was difficult. If only he taught the class! She gazed out the

191

window as she rested her fingers for a moment and saw Carson striding across the yard to the mailbox.

"Carson's back!" she hollered to her mother.

"At the mailbox again, I suppose?" Victoria asked.

"Yes, why?"

"He's there every afternoon hoping for another letter from that German woman."

"Does he get letters from her often?" Ava watched as Carson flipped through the envelopes. He must not have seen any to his liking, because he put them all back in the box and headed back out.

"Those two have become quite the pen pals," Victoria answered. "I don't think he knows that I know just how many letters he puts in that box and takes out of that box."

Ava watched her brother, with shoulders slouching, walk away and grinned. He was in love, but wasn't it a hopeless one?

A week later, Carson wasn't disappointed. A letter addressed to him in Maria's small print was waiting for him. He tucked it in his shirt pocket, put the other mail back in the box, and looked up to see if he saw his mother's face in the window. She wasn't to be seen, so he walked out a good distance from the house and sat down in the stubby grass. He studied Maria's handwriting of his name for a moment and then carefully opened the envelope that had come all the way from Germany just for him.

Dear Carson,

I am happy for you on the birth of your niece! Have you met her yet? We have not had a baby in our family for so long. New life is always to be treasured. Berty is thirteen now and still the baby in our family. He still behaves like a baby sometimes too! Mom says no to him little. But the war made him grow up. He has good manners and is learning to be the man of our family.

I have decided to go back to work. A Mrs. Gerda Meier has asked me to work for her. She is a friend of my mother and owns a bakery. I have never baked much, but she says that is of no matter. She says she will teach me everything there is to learn. Let's hope so! I will begin tomorrow.

I think that working will be good for me. It will help me get my mind off the past and look forward. Sometimes, I miss your Alabama. Being there made me forget all the terrible things that happened here and helped me to remember only the good. If only I could just remember the good all the time. Why is it so hard? It could be living among all the ruined buildings in Berlin. So much destruction everywhere! I wish the rebuilding would happen quicker. Sometimes, I think us women are the only ones who care about it. Albin did, but he was too tired and then didn't live long enough.

What are you speaking on this week? I have been trying to read my Bible more because of you, and the words are beginning to have new meaning for me. I used to find them old and empty as a child.

Take care of yourself.
Maria

Carson read the letter a second time and then tucked it back in his shirt pocket. He spent the rest of the afternoon thinking about what to write to her and finally pulled out a blank piece of paper and pen when he was alone in his bed late that night.

Dear Maria,

No, I haven't got to meet my niece yet. My parents did. They said she is a beauty and looks nothing like my brother. She is fair-headed and blue-eyed like her mother. I will meet her one day. Whenever my mother can manage to get them here again. I suppose I could visit Atlanta. Maybe I should have taken you to Atlanta when you were here. It's a big city. Probably not the size of your Berlin, but big.

You asked how to forget all the terrible things that have happened. I would read Psalms. David lived through betrayal, war…

Carson stopped and ripped up the letter. He wanted to be more to her than a pastor. It had to be personal and not a sermon. He pulled out a clean sheet of paper and re-wrote the first part of the letter then continued:

You asked how to forget all the terrible things that have happened. When I dwell on bad things, like when my sister-in-law died and how the war changed my brother, I remember John 16:33. Read it. The world will always be full of death and trouble, but in the end, God has overcome the world. It is the hope I cling to when I see or feel suffering. It helps to know this world is not the end. One day, if we know Christ, we'll go to a place with no more sorrow. I hope that helps you too. I haven't experienced the same heartaches you have, so to try to say anything that will help may be pointless.

You could always come back to Alabama! Maybe I'll speak on John 16:33 Sunday. You've inspired me.

Was the last sentence too much? His pen was still for a moment while he thought. He could hear Grandpa Chester snoring in the next room. He decided to leave it.

Your job sounds nice. What will you be baking? I am about to have more work than I want for a while. It's almost time to begin harvesting our cotton. Sure hope it cools off in the next couple of weeks. Cotton is hard enough without the hot sun beating down on you! Should have less cotton to harvest next year. We are planting soybean for the first time in the spring. What is the weather like in Berlin? Tell your aunt hello for me.

Carson

Chapter 36

The French Ambassador and his wife sat at the front, center table of the banquet hall. Ava and the rest of the girls, all dressed in matching, black dresses, looked down at them from the stage as they waited for the student orchestra to situate themselves behind them. Ambassador Bonnet wore a black suit and bow tie and had a large nose that hung down over a trimmed mustache. He smiled up at them with courteous expectation. Madame Bonnet sat beside him in a white, floor-length, satin gown. She also wore a pale pink corsage on her left breast which matched her pink lips and the beaded clip in her hair. Her hair was rolled back away from her bright face, which like her husband's smiled up with diplomatic interest. Seated around the Bonnets were Senator John Sparkman, Lieutenant Governor Clarence Inzer, Speaker of the House W.M. Beck, and other political and school dignitaries.

While most of the girls were nervous to be singing in front of these men of importance, Ava wasn't any more nervous than normal. Sure, she had the usual pre-performance jitters, but they would dissipate with the first note of music. The band had taught her how to sing in front of all sorts of people. The orchestra was ready and began to play.

"Alma Mater, Alma Mater, grateful voices raise a song of tribute and devotion," the girls sang. "Thy honored name we praise. Light of knowledge, store of wisdom, love of truth abide in thee. Quest for beauty, search from freedom, thine eternally. Oh, Alma Mater, Alma Mater, we humbly bow to thee!"

They finished the song in English, the orchestra played a short interlude, and they began again.

"Lieu ou l'on a fait ses etudes, reconnaissant voix lever," the girls sang in their rehearsed French. Ava loved the way her mouth and tongue moved to annunciate the new language. They finished the song, and the room erupted in applause. Ambassador and Madame Bonnet stood to their feet as they clapped, and the rest of the room followed suite. Mrs. Wheeler waved in gratitude to their audience and then ushered her choir off the stage and to the back of the room.

"Wonderful, just wonderful!" she whispered, hugging each of them. Ava hugged her back when it was her turn.

There were chairs waiting for them along the back wall. As they sat down, Senator John Sparkman welcomed the ambassador to the stage.

"Thank you. I am honored to be on your beautiful campus," Ambassador Bonnet said to the senator and then to his audience. "The Jacksonville State Teacher's College is truly a remarkable school. Last year, when my wife and I were told you had opened an International House for French students, we were greatly heartened. In these days following the war, it is important that we all work toward international brotherhood. Your college is nurturing both American and foreign students, which will make that possible."

He spoke more about the college and then turned his attention to world politics.

"By now, I am sure that most of you have heard of the Marshall Plan. Your Secretary of State, George Marshall, has proposed a plan to aid in the economic recovery of Western Europe. You may be wondering what that plan has to do with university students in Alabama. European stabilization is needed for political rest and economic stability for our world economy and the United States. Of course, this plan would greatly benefit my country and the country of the French students you have right here on your campus. I believe that France can regain its feet economically within three years if the Marshall Plan is put into action."

His speech broadened Ava's world as Edwin's and James's letters had during the war. As she listened, she longed to travel and sing around the world.

"The Marshall Plan is just another name for give all Americans' hard-earned money away," Grandpa Chester griped and spat out a lemon seed.

"As an ally, we have to help rebuild what was torn down," Sheffield said from where he sat on the porch swing next to his wife. They were all drinking freshly made lemonade and relaxing after a difficult day of picking cotton. Victoria's short legs swung up as her husband pushed them backward and forward with his bare feet.

"Umph," Grandpa Chester retorted.

"Ambassador Bennet said that France could recover from the war in three years with the Marshall Plan," Ava added. She was leaning back on Edwin as he gulped down his lemonade. All week, he had been working a full day at the pipe shop and then helping out with the cotton until dark.

"I'm glad we're helping France and Great Britain, but I do not understand giving money to Germany," Victoria said and then eyed her son, remembering his frequent letter writing to the last of those countries. Carson seemed nonplussed. He was lying on his back and staring up at the night sky, his empty lemonade glass beside him.

"There are political reasons too," Edwin spoke. He was beginning to read the newspapers just as much as his father-in-law.

"I don't think any political reason is good enough to send money to those who were killing American soldiers just a couple of years ago." Victoria eyed her son again, but he didn't move, and she wondered if he was even listening to them or thinking about that widow again.

"Many are afraid that if we don't help Germany rebuild the Soviet Union could make it into another communist nation. It's a fight for political freedom as much as economic recovery," Sheffield explained.

Everyone was quiet for a moment. Ava loved to listen to her parents banter. Her mother always spoke from her heart, and her father always spoke from his head. Together, they usually found a balance on most matters.

"What difference does Germany being a communist nation make to us?"

"Much. I'm afraid that the world is now being divided into two camps, the Soviet, communist one and ours. It would be good to have as many on our side as possible."

"You're not talking about another war?" Victoria stamped one foot on the floor and stilled the swing.

"Preposterous!" Grandpa Chester spoke up again. "The world's in no shape for another war."

199

"I think you're right. Let's hope so," Sheffield replied.

Silence fell on the porch again as they each, except for Carson, contemplated what another war would look like.

"Going to bed," Carson broke the silence. Actually, he had been writing another letter to Maria in his head, and he was ready to put it down on paper.

Chapter 37

Rosemary spread out all the recipes her mother had sent her on the kitchen table. Sweet potato soufflé, pecan pie, chocolate pie, dressing, corn pudding," she read with her hands on her hips.

"Turkey first, then pies, then potatoes, then all the rest," she said out loud.

"You're going to work yourself silly," Percy said from behind her, and she jumped. It was very early in the morning, and she thought he was still in the bed.

"What are you doing in the kitchen?"

"Checking on you. I don't know why you wouldn't let Annamae help with all this."

"Annamae doesn't like to cook, and for the first time, I have this kitchen all to myself. I'm going to make you the best Thanksgiving dinner you've ever had."

"Just don't kill yourself in your present condition." He smiled down at her but didn't hug her. She was already pulling out a big roasting pan from the cabinet.

"I've been walking every day. I think I can cook a meal. Go back to bed." She shooed him away.

It was true about the walking. Since she had little house work to do, she had decided to take long walks every day to keep herself fit for the baby. Mrs. Ramsey agreed with her saying that it would be good for "her constitution." When she mentioned this to Percy, he just laughed and said her constitution was "just like it was supposed to be, perfect." Baby aside, it was fun to have the Ramsey's large kitchen all to herself and the opportunity to cook for her husband, who rarely wanted to stay home and eat.

When the turkey was in the stove, she turned her attention to the pecan pie. She poured a large mass of pecans out on the counter and began pounding them with a mallet. Despite all the walking, her breathing shallowed, and she was glad Percy had left. The pecans now in pieces, she pushed them aside and began to sprinkle flour out on the counter to roll out the pie crust she had made the day before. She stirred, chopped, and cooked right up until the moment their guests arrived.

"Welcome!" Percy greeted as if the house were theirs.

Rosemary quickly looked over the full table and then smoothed down her hair and dress, hoping her appearance looked as acceptable as the food.

"You've outdone yourself!" Annamae said when she saw the table. Johnny walked in behind her and then Percy's friend Ralph.

"Looks delicious," Johnny said.

"Maybe, I should get a wife!" Ralph joked, and they all laughed. He was a burly sort of man with hair all over, and Rosemary felt again that she might not like him. "Percy, you're a lucky man."

"I know," Percy replied and winked at his wife. "Let's sit down and eat."

They all sat down, and Rosemary did too after surveying the table one last time to be sure she hadn't forgotten the salt, pepper, and butter.

"I'll say grace," Percy said and reached for Rosemary's hand under the table. She squeezed it. It was nice to see him remember the blessing.

"Lord, thank you for this food. Thank you for my wife who prepared it, and thank you for these friends we have to share it with. Amen."

"Amen," Ralph seconded and began helping himself to the bowl of corn pudding in front of him.

"It must be nice to have this big place all to yourself for the week," Annamae said. "Where did you say the Ramseys are?"

"Visiting their nephew in Wisconsin," Rosemary answered. As she watched them fill their plates, all her efforts of the day hit her at once and she felt as her dad would say "old dog tired." Her arms and hands fell limp in her lap.

"Aren't you going to eat?" Percy asked.

"Just letting you all get to it first."

"Nonsense, here," he said and placed a large spoonful of sweet potato soufflé on her plate.

"I can't eat that much."

"You need it."

"He's right," Annamae agreed. "You're feeding two now. That's one part of pregnancy I'll enjoy."

"What?" Johnny asked, his own forkful of sweet potatoes hanging in the air.

"Not now! Don't worry."

Rosemary ate, but with every mouthful, she felt herself getting more and more tired, and she had to keep stifling yawns behind her napkin. They finished eating, and Annamae helped her clear off the table to play Rook. The men and Annamae smoked as they played the card game, and Rosemary felt like even the smell of it was making her nauseous this time, but she hid this as well.

"Pie?" she asked once another game had ended, wanting to fill their mouths with more than cigarettes.

"You don't have to ask me twice!" Johnny threw his cards down on the table and leaned back in his chair.

"I brought something to go with the pie," Ralph said and the left table as Annamae took orders of who wanted pecan pie and who wanted chocolate pie for her.

Rosemary was cutting the last piece, a slice of chocolate for herself, when Ralph returned with a brown paper bag. Her heart sank, and she looked down so no one would notice the glare intended for her husband's friend. She had been so proud of Percy for not mentioning anything about alcohol at their Thanksgiving meal.

"I knew there was a reason we invited you!" Percy laughed, pulling out a bottle of bourbon from the bag. "I'll get glasses."

He began pouring glasses for everyone but his wife.

"Oh no, not me today," Annamae said and smiled at Rosemary.

"Then more for us." Percy grinned.

The men drank and talked about work while Annamae told her about her family's Thanksgiving celebrations in South Carolina.

"We have so many relatives come to my Granny Frannie's house that you can't find a place where someone isn't sitting inside or outside. My mom and my aunts all help cook. Nan better have helped out this year and spared Mom some trouble! Seems like her butcher husband could have provided the turkey or ham himself."

Rosemary had been so busy that she hadn't paused to think about what she was missing with her own family today. She was sure they were all at Sheffield and Victoria's house, probably eating pies like the ones she had made and making music. Victoria loved to play her piano, and her dad and cousins loved to sing. Her mother would be singing too, but she just wasn't blessed with the "musical ear." Judith was probably up to something when they weren't paying her any attention.

I'll have to add more turkey broth next time. She was now thinking about how her dressing turned out drier than her mother's dressing.

The men got louder as the evening went on, and Rosemary hoped their neighbors wouldn't tell the Ramseys how loud their house had been while they were away.

"We can eat a leftover turkey sandwich and a slice of pie before we leave in the morning," Annamae said.

"We have plenty of bread," Rosemary replied and noticed as she did how the house had gotten quieter. The men were still talking but in lower voices.

"The worst I saw was a man who was clear blown in two," she heard Ralph say.

"Worst I saw was a poor chap whose arm had been blown off. Believe it or not, he was running around looking for that arm," Johnny said and then laughed.

"Did he find it?" Percy asked.

"Don't think it mattered."

They were silent for a moment and then it was Percy's turn.

"For me, it would have to be a soldier I saw blow his own brains out."

"Shot himself?" Ralph asked.

"Fear. He couldn't take the constant fear anymore. Always wondered what they told the family."

"Isn't it amazing how they can talk to each other about all that stuff and not us?" Annamae whispered, and Rosemary realized that she had been listening too.

"I didn't know he had seen something that horrible." Rosemary felt a little sick now and more tired than she had all night.

"They all did."

It wasn't long until the men were loud and laughing again, and the next thing Rosemary remembered was Percy carrying her upstairs to their bed.

Chapter 38

Now that the holiday season was here again, everyone wanted to hear music. Fort Payne, Huntsville, Albertville, and Montgomery – the Willie Harold Band had been all over the state spreading Christmas cheer. Tonight was Auburn, and once again, they had left on the bus before Edwin could get off work in time to join them. Ava dreaded another night in a hotel room without him.

They were playing at Auburn University, and the college students were rowdier than their usual crowds. The dance floor was filled with more people than Ava had ever seen, but somehow, everyone still found room to move to the music. The students' energy transferred to the band. Their sound was vibrant but brash, and Ava felt that she had to "sing from her gut" more as her cousin Jude would put it.

"When you wake on Christmas morn, the little boy blue will blow his horn. The three little bears will beat the drums in the Dixieland Band from Santa Claus land," Ava belted out. "You'll see Santa leading the band with a great, big peppermint stick. And if you behave, by jiminy, they'll come marching down your chimney! Gee what a Christmas it will be, a Dixieland band beneath your tree. You'll see all your toy-time pals and chums in the Dixieland band from Santa Claus land."

There was a brief pause, and Ava spoke rather than sang, "It was the night before Christmas and quiet as a mouse, but listen to the saxophone in J.D.'s house!"

Their saxophone player, Clifford, took the lead, and Ava stood beside him clapping her hips and bobbing her head. Once again, she felt electrified by the music, and it showed in the heightened color of her cheeks, which matched her red, holiday dress and lipstick.

The song ended and another immediately filled the room until the night was late. Willie Harold wished all the students a good night and a Merry Christmas, and the tired band packed up and left to retire to their hotel rooms.

"Ava!" someone called out as soon as she stepped out into the cool December air. She looked up and into the face of her husband. He was grinning and standing in front of a car she didn't recognize.

"What are you doing here?" She ran to him and flung her arms around him.

"I came in your Christmas present." He held his cold cheek against her warm one.

"What are you talking about?" She pulled away from him and looked around. He stood aside, and she now fully saw the beige Chevrolet with a dark brown top.

"Merry Christmas!" he said and laughed at her surprise.

"This is ours?" She looked from the car to him and back to the car.

"Sure is. We finally saved enough, and now, I can come to all your performances."

Ava ran her hand over the car's hood.

"Our very own car. Can I drive it?" she asked, clapping her hands together.

"Of course!"

She embraced him again and laughed thinking of what her mother would say when she saw her behind the wheel. She was older than when James first got his car, and her mother couldn't forbid her from driving her very own car!

In the days that followed, Edwin helped Ava get her driver's license, and they took turns driving down every dirt and paved road they could find. Since Victoria couldn't say anything beyond a disapproving look about her daughter driving, she chose to just ignore the car altogether. Sheffield, Carson, and even Grandpa Chester fawned over it, but Victoria stayed away from it and any mention of it. She couldn't look over it, though, when they drove it over on Christmas Day to show James, Vivie, and her husband's parents.

"Everyone knows what a car looks like!" Victoria said where her daughter could hear.

"Nothing beats the beauty of a brand new car," Jack Stilwell disagreed, inspecting one of the front wheels.

"Spoken like a true man!" Vivie said and laughed one of her monstrous laughs.

"Nonsense, nothing can beat the face of a new baby," Lavenia Stilwell spoke up. She for one wasn't looking at the car but at the five month-old infant in her arms. "Isn't that right now, Jacqueline?" She asked of the little girl peeping up at the strange face of the woman holding her. Jacqueline was bundled up in a blanket so tight that all you could make out of her were her wide, blue eyes and tiny, pinched nose.

"Yes, we should all be inside playing with these babies and not out in the cold gawking at a car," Victoria said. She was standing beside her mother-in-law with Ella in her arms.

"Pretty car!" Ella squealed and clung close to her grandmother for warmth.

"Remember that time you two got hold of the keys to my new car and drove it without asking?" James looked at Ava and Carson and grinned.

"We had all sorts of fun doing circles in the dirt!" Carson laughed.

"Ok, James, payback time. I'll let you drive mine!" Ava punched her oldest brother in the arm.

"After lunch, then. Let's see where I can find some mud!"

"There's some out behind the barn," Sheffield offered.

"Dad!" Ava protested, and they all laughed.

"Edwin might have something to say about that," Carson said.

"As long as James helps wash it up, I'm in!" Edwin replied.

Victoria and Lavenia turned to take the kids back inside, and they all followed. The house was warm and snug feeling and all dressed for the holidays. Victoria put Ella down, and the little girl ran to her aunt.

"Auntie drive?" she asked, tugging at Ava's dress.

"Yes, I do," Ava answered hesitantly and twirled the toddler around by the hand. She might not be afraid of her mother, but she was afraid of her grandmother.

"I'm all for women driving," Lavenia declared, and Ava could feel her mother's stunned silence behind her. "After seeing the way men drive in Birmingham, I think we'd all be better off if women did the driving."

"Lavenia, you can't be serious!" her husband said and sat down beside her and the baby.

"I am serious, and you are part of the reason why!"

"Me?"

"Yes, you. Sheffield, you should see the way your father drives sometimes. He's always trying to drive and talk to people he passes on the sidewalk at the same time."

Now that, Ava could imagine of her congenial grandfather.

"Again!" Ella squealed, and Ava kept twirling her around by her fingertips. The red and green bows in her chestnut hair flew up as she spun, and Ava laughed at her merriment.

Jacqueline began crying, and Lavenia moved the baby expertly to her shoulder.

"There, there, now," Lavenia said and patted her back gingerly. "Is my baby hungry?"

"I'm sure she is. I'll go feed her." Vivie held out her hands, and Lavenia gently placed the crying infant in them. "She just wants to eat all the time."

"Thriving babies do that," Lavenia replied, and Vivie moved to the corner of the room to feed Jacqueline under her blanket.

"How are your studies coming along?" Jack asked.

Ava looked up but realized her grandfather was talking to James, and she supposed Georgia Tech was more prominent in his mind than the Jacksonville State Teacher's College.

211

"Good, but more work than I imagined," James answered.

"He studies all night. Never sleeps. Of course, no one in our family does anymore except for Ella," Vivie said from the corner and laughed.

So, Vivie has discovered his habit of staying up all night, Ava thought. Her brother did have a worn look about his eyes and forehead, but he seemed to have come back from the war that way.

"Hard work always bring progress." Jack nodded approvingly. "There will be plenty of time to sleep later."

James smiled in response, but Ava wondered if he would ever be able to sleep soundly again.

"Are your studies tiring you out too?" Lavenia turned to Ava.

"No, I believe I have more time than James," Ava answered.

"She does, but what has been tiring her out is that band," Victoria said. "She's been singing all month all over the state."

"Is that so?" Jack beamed at his granddaughter, and Ava smiled under his gaze.

"And what have you been up to?" Lavenia now turned to Carson, determined to check on the state of all her grandchildren.

"Just preaching and farming," Carson muttered from the floor. Ella was sitting in his lap now and playing with stacking blocks.

"And writing to his new acquaintances in Germany," Victoria added, and Ava swallowed down a laugh at her brother's face, which had turned as red as a tomato.

212

"Germany!" Lavenia exclaimed. "Who can you possibly know in Germany?"

"One of the German POWs I supervised during the war passed away, and his widow and aunt came to visit the fort," Carson explained, but he kept his eyes on the lettered blocks he was stacking into the shape of a pyramid for his niece.

"I hope they were pleased with their visit. I always thought we treated those POWs a little too well during the war. Our poor men were not treated the same."

"Many feel that way, but we did the right thing," Carson replied. "We treated them as God would have us treat our enemies." Just then Ella knocked over the pyramid, and everyone laughed as she cried over what she had purposively knocked over a moment ago.

"I'll rebuild it," Carson told her.

Jude, Myrtle, and Judith arrived, and Victoria, Ava, and Vivie served Christmas lunch. Usually, Jude and Myrtle kept to their own family on Christmas day, but they missed Rosemary, and Victoria thought that being around more people might help to lessen the pain. When they had feasted, they lounged about the living room waiting for Victoria to strike up her piano.

"Want to hold her?" Vivie asked Ava and looked down at Jacqueline who was asleep in her arms.

"Would it wake her?" Ava replied.

"Oh no, she can sleep as soundly as your Grandpa Chester when she's being held." Just then, Grandpa Chester let out a snore from his rocking chair, and they giggled.

"Then, yes." Ava held out her arms and took the baby. Her head moved slightly from side to side, and her eyelids fluttered for a moment, but she didn't wake. The blanket was looser now about her head, and Ava could make out blond wisps of hair. They were so light that she almost looked bald. Her face was round and serene, and Ava wondered what she could possibly be dreaming about. For the first time, she also wondered what her baby would have looked like. Would he or she have had dark hair like her or more auburn hair like Edwin?

"It must be nice to be unbothered by everything," Ava whispered to Vivie and pushed the thought of her own baby out of her head. It was Christmas, and she didn't want to think about anything sad.

"I know, no household duties, jobs, studies, bills," Vivie said and sighed.

"Ok, Mom, time to make music," James called out. "I brought my banjo!"

Soon the house was loud with all their voices, but the baby just kept sleeping in Ava's arms. Ava looked into her face and saw the "peace on earth" they sang about.

Chapter 39

New Year's Day 1948 was quieter at the Stilwells. Victoria had come down with a rare cold and was in the bed, and Ava was in charge of cooking the black-eyed peas, collards, and corn bread. Even though her mother firmly preached that "all blessings came from the Lord," she insisted that they eat the traditional New Year's Day meal to help ensure that their crops were good in the upcoming year. Ava pulled the heavy skillet of cornbread out of the oven and set it down on the stove next to the peas and collards.

"It's all ready," she announced to her husband, dad, brother, and grandpa.

No one answered. They were too busy listening to the Sugar Bowl to pay her or their stomachs any attention at the moment. Alabama was playing Texas in New Orleans. She sat down on the couch between her husband and brother and listened with them. Even though Edwin was from Tennessee, her family had quickly converted him into an Alabama fan, and she laughed at the studious expression on his face as he too listened to the radio commentators announce completed and uncompleted passes, tackles, and yards gained.

"And the pass from Gilmer is good. White has the ball. Touchdown Alabama! Touchdown Alabama!" the announcer screamed through the radio, and Sheffield jumped up with a fist in the air.

"Told you Harry Gilmer wouldn't let us down," Grandpa Chester said and settled back in his rocking chair as if he had known the touchdown would happen all along.

"Even the best don't have a good game every time," Sheffield replied. It was halftime, and the men hurried to the kitchen for a quick bite to eat before the game resumed.

"Peas for pennies, greens for dollars, and cornbread for gold," Grandpa Chester muttered, and Edwin laughed. He hadn't grown up hearing her grandpa say the same thing every New Year's Day the way she and Carson had.

"Think I'll see if Mom feels like a plate," Ava said and left them.

She slowly opened the door to her mother's room. Victoria was so far down in the covers that she could have been mistaken for a lump of pillows.

"Mom," Ava called in a soft voice.

Victoria stirred and lowered her covering.

"What's wrong?" she asked. Her eyes were watery, and her black hair was a mess about her head.

"Nothing, just thought you might like a bite to eat."

"No, not now," Victoria replied and let her eyes close again.

"But you haven't eaten anything today. You always tell us that a body can't fight to get better without a little nourishment."

"Alright, then." Victoria sighed and began propping herself up on her pillows.

"I'll go get a plate for you," Ava said. "Besides, you wouldn't want to be responsible for a bad crop this year."

"I said alright. You got me." Victoria gave her daughter's or rather her own argument a half smile.

216

Ava returned with the plate and sat by her mother as she ate.

"Feeling any better?" she asked.

"A little. Too congested to sleep last night but too tired today not too." Victoria swallowed a bite of peas, and Ava passed her a glass of sweet tea to wash it down with.

"What are the men up to?"

"Can't you guess?"

"Oh, that football game," Victoria said and made herself take another bite. "Is Bama winning?"

"I think it was tied at the half."

"Well, I hope they win for all our sakes. Your dad and grandpa get all out of sorts when Alabama loses."

"I'm afraid Edwin might too." Ava laughed. "Hopefully, he'll get to finish the game with them. We have to leave in a couple of hours for Montgomery."

"Be careful." Victoria pointed her fork at her daughter.

"We'll drive careful," Ava replied, trying to keep the annoyance she felt out of her voice.

"Not really about the driving...about everything." Victoria passed her half-eaten plate back to her daughter and began nestling herself back down in her covers.

"Always do. Goodnight or good afternoon, whatever you like." Ava stood up with the plate and left her mother to rest, wondering what all dangers she reckoned might overtake her.

After halftime, the game didn't go in Alabama's favor. Gilmer was having one of the worst games of his college career, and the team was making error after error.

"You shouldn't have said that about Gilmer not having a good game every time. You may have jinxed him," Grandpa Chester grumbled.

"It's not just Gilmer," Sheffield returned and ran his fingers through his hair in frustration.

"We're practically giving them the game!" Carson said and slapped his leg as another bad play was called out.

They were all four getting grumpy, and Ava decided she had had enough.

"Going to get ready," she told Edwin and kissed him on the cheek.

"I'll be right there," he replied.

None of the rest said a word to her as the word "fumble" came through the radio, and they all groaned together.

She left them to their game and readied herself for her next performance. Soon enough, Edwin was back and, indeed, not in the best of moods. The adventure of driving their new car over two hours away changed his outlook, however.

The Montgomery crowd was older than their last crowd, but the holiday champagne made them just as rowdy as the night went on. Ava sang and watched from the stage as they danced the New Year in. She was glad when she had a break to dance herself and almost ran down the stage steps to find Edwin.

"Whoa, slow down," a man she almost ran into halted her. He had meticulously styled brown hair and wore a sleek black suit that seemed to shine in the lights from the stage.

"Excuse me," Ava said. She started to run past him, but he just stood there smiling at her as if she knew him from somewhere.

"You know with your voice you could do better," he said.

"What do you mean?" she asked, still trying to figure out if she knew him or not. *Was he a former band member?*

"You really have no idea who I am, do you?" he asked in return.

"I'm so sorry, but no."

"Elliot King," he said and held out his hand.

"Oh, Mr. King! Of course, I've heard of you," Ava stammered and shook his hand.

"I've heard about you too. Everybody in the band world has."

"They have? I can't believe that." Ava gave him a disbelieving look, and he laughed.

"Those that matter have. I've been listening to you sing all night. You belong in a bigger band, Ava."

"I'm right where I belong, Mr. King," she replied, taken aback by a man like Elliot King knowing her name. He was a band leader like Willie Harold but of a larger, more nationally known band.

"I'm out a lead female singer right now. Janene is having a baby, and I've got a string of concerts coming up in the south. I want you to take her place for a while. What do you think?"

Ava just stood there, unable to believe what was being asked of her. She had heard Janene Richman on the radio. Janene was a true big band singer with a voice as powerful as any instrument.

"If you're worried about Willie, I'll talk to him. He can spare you for a little while. He wouldn't want you not to have this opportunity.

"I don't know if I'm good enough to fill in for Janene Richman," Ava admitted with a blush.

"You are after what I heard tonight. You're every bit as good as she is," he replied, and she blushed again. "Just don't tell her I said that."

"I also have school. I'm in college."

"We'll work around it."

She smiled now, her head spinning with the possibility.

"How would I practice?"

"We'll send you the music and practice before performances."

"Ava," Edwin called from behind her, and she took his hand.

"Mr. King, this is my husband, Edwin."

"A pleasure to meet you." The bandleader shook Edwin's hand. "Your wife is very talented."

"Thank you. She is," he replied, but Ava could tell he was wondering who the man complimenting his wife was.

"I'm another bandleader," Elliot went on, reading Edwin as well. "I'm offering your wife a temporary place in our band for the next few months. We play in larger venues than Willie's band does, so she would be growing her audience."

"That's quite an offer," Edwin said and squeezed Ava's hand. "She deserves it."

"I was just telling Mr. King that I wouldn't want to quit on Willie or interrupt my cla...."

"Of course," Elliot interrupted. "We wouldn't want her to do that. I'll pay her $50.00 a week to take the bus and meet us where we're singing each weekend. She won't miss any classes. We'll play all songs with a male lead during any weekday performances.

Ava felt Edwin's hand jerk. Fifty dollars was a lot of money.

"Make it $65.00 to cover her bus fare," Elliot offered.

"We own a car," Ava said.

"Then use the extra for gas."

"I still need to think about it, Mr. King. I don't want to put Willie out."

"Willie's a good guy. He'll understand you taking a few months break."

"I don't know."

"It can't hurt anything for Mr. King to speak to him about it," Edwin said to her. "You've worked hard for this."

She looked at them both and bit her bottom lip, contemplating Elliot's persuasive offer and Edwin's pride in her.

"Alright, then," she agreed, giving in more to her husband.

"Great!" Elliot said. "I'll be in touch then through Willie. He's an old friend and a good chum. I'll work everything out. Now, you two go dance before you're needed back up on that stage,"

"Thank you, Mr. King," Ava replied.

"Call me Elliot."

"Very nice to meet you," Edwin said.

The two men shook hands again, and Edwin pulled her onto the dance floor she had been eagerly waiting for all night.

Chapter 40

Percy took Rosemary's hand and pulled her out of the car, belly first.

"I hate being so cumbersome," she groaned. The cold, northern air actually felt good as it rushed into her lungs.

"I like you as a bigger woman." Percy grinned down at her.

"Stop it." Rosemary laughed as he now helped her up the small flight of steps to the porch. "You're just saying that to make me feel better, and you know it."

"I'll never admit to that!" He laughed with her, digging for his key in his pants pocket.

"Can we just sit on the porch a minute?"

"Rosemary, it is twenty degrees out here!"

"We're wearing coats," she pleaded and fell back onto the swing.

"All right, anything for you." He sat down next to her.

They swung up, and she loved the way it made her feel weightless even in her present state. A muted mingle of distant cars and Mrs. Ramsey's radio filled the silence.

"Sitting in this swing always reminds me of home," Rosemary said.

"You're not homesick are you?" he asked in what sounded like a hurt voice to her.

"No, but I do miss them. Don't you miss your family?"

"I guess, sometimes, but my family isn't like yours."

"I'm sure they miss you," she said, and he chuckled.

"No, I don't think they miss me, but I love how you always think the best of people."

"I think you're wrong." She put an arm through his and leaned in closer. "Wouldn't it be fun to take the baby back south for a visit this summer. He or she could meet my parents and Samuel?" His body stiffened at the sound of his son's name.

"I'm not ready to go back to Savannah. I don't want to interrupt Samuel's life again, and do you honestly think your parents want to see me, the man who took their daughter from them?"

"If I love you, they will. You just have to give them a chance."

He started to speak but then stopped, and they sat in silence again listening to the faint hum of the radio.

"We'll see," he finally said, and Rosemary hugged his arm. "After you go to bed, I'm going to go have a drink with Ralph. You don't mind, do you?"

"Of course not," she lied, glad that her head was on his shoulder and he couldn't see her face.

"I don't want you out late anymore in your condition. We have to be careful now," he said, and she knew he had guessed her thoughts and was trying to soothe her.

"Ok, but don't be gone too long." She now looked up at him and was assured by the love she saw in his face, the face that hadn't been drinking yet.

"I can't stay away from you that long!" He stood and pulled her up from the swing. "Come on. Let's get you and the baby inside."

Later that night, Rosemary woke up. Her size and the pressure of the baby often woke her up. She couldn't sleep on her stomach, the way she preferred, and if she laid on her back, she became uncomfortable. She moved begrudgingly onto her side and realized that Percy was still not back. She reached for his pocket watch on the night stand.

"It's after two o'clock. Why isn't he back yet?" she whispered to the darkness.

She lay there listening, hoping to hear his footsteps on the staircase. Her fears and their conversation on the swing kept her awake. She did miss her family, more than she would ever let Percy know. As it got closer and closer for her baby to be born, she missed her mother more and more. She never dreamed that when she had a baby her own mother wouldn't be there to help and witness the first breaths. Sure, she had Mrs. Ramsey and Annamae, but it wasn't the same. Tears ran across her face and fell on her pillow. Now, she did hear footsteps on the stairs. The front door opened, and Percy stumbled in. She closed her eyes tightly and pretended to be asleep. She didn't want to see him after he had been drinking anyway.

Chapter 41

Her first music from Elliot King had arrived! Ava didn't even wait to get the package back to the porch to tear through the envelope.

" 'It's Magic,' 'My Happiness,' and 'The Wonder of You,' " she read through the song selections when the bundle of sheet music was in her hands.

She couldn't wait to pound out the notes and begin committing the lyrics to memory. Every time she received a new song, she liked to have it memorized before the next practice. She placed the music carefully back in the envelope and began running to her parents' house.

Maybe, once I start getting paid from Elliot King, we can buy a piano! If they could save up and buy a car, surely they could save up for a piano. She was so busy thinking about having her own piano that she almost missed Carson sauntering away from the mailbox again. He had obviously received what he had been hoping for too by the silly smile that was spread across his face.

"Did you win a contest?" Ava called out, and he jumped like she had spooked him.

"What are you doing here?" he asked instead of answering.

"Need to practice on the piano."

"Well, get to it," he said and hurried away with the letter that had given him such a smile.

When he was sure his sister was no longer anywhere close, he sat down on the crunchy, cold ground and opened the envelope that was once again addressed to him in Maria's handwriting.

Dear Carson,

I did it! I made my first good Black Forest Cake, and it was wonderful. Everyone at the bakery said so. Even Mrs. Meier praised it! Have you ever heard of Black Forest Cake in America? It has layers of chocolate sponge cake, cream, cherries, kirschwasser, and chocolate pieces. My cake was five layers! I wish you could have tasted it. It is nice to have cake again. There were no cakes during the war. Are the women in your church still baking you cakes? What is your favorite?

Things here in Berlin are still not peaceful. The Soviets, the Americans, and the British are fighting over control of the city. I am thankful that we are in the western sector and not the Soviet one. I wish I never had to see a Soviet soldier again in my life! Some here think that there may be another war over control of Berlin and Germany. I hope not. I don't think this city could survive another war. Have you heard anything about it in America?

Aunt Bernadette is traveling again. She left yesterday to go back to England for a month. She still has family there. I wish I could have gone with her, but I do have work now. Mother needs me too. She is worried about Berty. He doesn't think he needs to go back to school. One day Germany will be strong again, and his education will be needed. Pray for him.

227

Pray that he will see that our reasoning is good. I know God hears your prayers.

Take care of yourself.

Maria

Carson folded and then hid the letter in his shirt pocket. He was sure his father and grandpa were missing him now. They were used to his afternoon disappearances, but he didn't want to leave them with all the work that had to be done before dinner.

Another war? Impossible! He thought but then remembered his parents and grandpa discussing the Marshall Plan a while ago. He would have to start reading more than just the Bible and Maria's letters and pay attention to political things. Above all, he just wished he could bring Maria back to Alabama and protect her from all the unrest around her.

When it came time to wash up for dinner, Ava was still there playing the piano and singing to herself. He supposed she and Edwin were eating with them tonight.

"What's for dinner?" he poked his head in the kitchen and asked his mother.

"Chicken livers," Victoria answered.

"Sounds good," Carson said, and his stomach growled in agreement. He started to leave her and then poked his head back in. "Ever heard of Black Forest Cake?"

"No, not that I can recall." Victoria thought as she wiped her hands on her apron. "Why? Did one of those church ladies make it for you?"

"Nope, just heard of it." Carson rushed off before she could ask any more questions.

"Black Forest Cake," he heard his mother muttering behind him.

"Maybe you should have Mom play that song for you so you can hear the real notes," Carson said to his sister as he passed by her, and she gave him the nasty look he was hoping for.

Dear Maria,

My favorite cake is my mom's chocolate cake. She makes it for all our birthdays. I wish I could have tried your Black Forest Cake. You will have to make it for me if I ever see you again.   Mrs. Faulkner made me a carrot cake this week. I brought it home, and my grandpa ate most of it. Mom said it wasn't moist enough.

I will pray for Bertie. Yes, God hears my prayers. He also hears yours. David tells us in Psalms 34 that the Lord's ears are attentive to the righteous. I always think of that and my behavior when I question whether or not God hears my prayers. I'm sorry. I didn't mean to send you a sermon. I think it's in my blood.

I haven't heard anything about another war over Germany, but I do know that the United States and the Soviet Union are not on the best of terms. Their quarrel is over political beliefs. I personally don't think any country wants another war right now. Too many lives have already been lost. The United States has greatly reduced the size of its army.

It's getting late. I guess I need to go to bed. What are you learning to bake next?

Carson

Chapter 42

Ava stood staring at the stage. It was twice as big as any she had performed on before, and Elliot King's band filled the back half of it from curtain to curtain.

"Fellows, meet our new gal singer!" Elliot announced, and they all clapped for her. A couple even hooted.

"It's a true honor to be here," Ava said, nodding appreciatively. "Thank you for having me. I hope I don't disappoint you."

"'she breathed a little easier under his confidence.

"Let's get right to it boys and gal. Seven o'clock will be here before we know it." Elliot shuffled the music on his stand. "'It's Magic' first. Ready, Ava?"

"Yes," she said and turned away from the band toward the almost empty room. Edwin was sitting up front and center, and his warm gaze steadied her.

The sound that came from the band was enormous. It wasn't hard to find her cue, and before she had time to doubt herself any longer, she was singing with the band.

"You sigh, a song begins," she sang out uninhibited now, like the instruments behind her, "You speak, and I hear violins. It's magic."

A few short hours later, she was singing the same song with an audience much bigger.

"Why do I tell myself these things that happen are all really true when in my heart I know that the magic is my love for you," she sang, and the last note played.

She looked up at Elliot, who was now by her side, and he beamed down at her in approval.

"Ladies and gentlemen, let's give a big hand for Ms. Ava Livingston. This is her first night with our band."

The room erupted with applause, and she gave a little bow. Elliot took her by the hand and led her to a stool just to the right of the stage.

"Thank you," she whispered, and he squeezed her hand.

"You were perfect," he replied before hurrying back to his place.

"Now, for an older hit that I know you Mississippians are sure to love," he teased, and the audience gave him another applause before they even heard the first note of the song he was speaking of.

Everyone was clapping again the moment the band began playing, and Ava recognized Count Basie's "One O'Clock Jump." Why Mississippians would love the song any more than Alabamians or Georgians or anyone else for that matter, she didn't know, but they were into it, dancing, swaying, and watching Elliot's every move. She too watched Elliot, who was one minute directing, one minute playing his trombone, and one minute playing up to the audience. He was certainly the star of his own show. His onstage energy surpassed Willie Harold's by a mile. Ava sang three more songs with the band before the night ended. When their performance was over, many in the crowd were up at the stage with them.

231

"Elliot, you should keep this one," an older man in a tuxedo with his arm around a much younger woman nodded toward her and said.

"I will if she'll let me." Elliot winked in her direction. Ava smiled in return as Edwin joined them. More came up as well, and Ava noticed that most of them were women waiting for their turn with Elliot.

"See you next weekend in Louisiana?" a heavy-set clarinet player asked.

"You bet," she answered.

"Name's Ollie," he said and extended his hand to first her and then Edwin.

"Edwin." Edwin met his handshake. "You all did some good playing up there tonight."

"Thanks, man," Ollie replied. "Will you be in Louisiana too?"

"Wouldn't miss it."

Later that night, Ava lay next to Edwin in their hotel room thinking about her successful night.

"Do you ever get tired of hearing me sing?"

"Never," he replied and moved closer to her. "You're my Songbird."

She smiled in the darkness at the name he had begun calling her in his letters home from the war. How long ago it all seemed at this moment.

"Do you think Carson intends to do something about that German woman?" she asked, not knowing why that suddenly came to her mind.

"I don't see how, but we need to get to sleep now. We have a five-hour drive home tomorrow."

"All right," she answered as she imagined what all could be in those letters her brother sent back and forth from Germany.

Edwin's grip around her loosened, and Ava knew he was asleep.

The next weekend, Ava and Edwin had an even father drive to join the band in Baton Rouge, LA. The miles went by quickly as they imagined going to even farther away places and snacked on sandwiches and cookies.

When they arrived, Ava had another surprise. A male singer named Lonny Sands was already warming up with the band.

"Good timing!" Elliot exclaimed when he saw her. "We were just getting to your part." He placed a page of sheet music in her hands and just like that she was singing her first professional duet.

Lonny was a small man with a melodic voice that seemed to ripple in the air with each note.

"I'd want to marry him today," she sang.

"But you don't say who," he sang back.

"That I cannot do," she sang again.

"Happen to be me?"

"Possibly."

They went back and forth until the chorus.

"Love somebody, but I won't say who," they now sang together.

The song ended, and the band clapped.

"Natural together!" Elliot praised. "From the top again."

They practiced the song a few more times, and another concert was underway. Ava sang by herself, they sang together, and Lonny sang by himself. She loved watching another soloist work and admired his engaging composure. He had a way of making each person feel like he was singing directly to them, and when they were singing together, she marveled at his acting just as much as his singing. It was as though he meant every word he sang, no matter how absurd, and she was afraid at first that Edwin would be jealous. Lonny was also a married man from Tennessee, however, and the two of them got along like forgotten cousins. Soon, they were going for coffee together after shows. Sometimes, other band members or Elliot would join them, but mostly it was just the three of them. The rest usually preferred a drink stronger than coffee.

"Give yourselves some time before you have any kids," Lonny said to them one night over coffee and pie. Ava's heart faltered, and Edwin's body stiffened beside her.

"Marianne used to travel with me to my concerts too before the babies came. Love them to death, but they take up all your extra time and money once you have them," Lonny continued when neither of them said anything.

"How did you get started singing?" Edwin asked, and Ava smiled at her husband's love for her.

"In Nashville, everyone thinks they can sing. I just really could. Moved up like Ava from band to band. Also, look at me. I don't think God made my body for hard labor. The Army didn't even want me!" He laughed at his own physique.

Ava sat up straight at his words. *Is that what I'm doing? Am I too moving up in the music world?* Edwin and Lonny kept talking, but Ava didn't hear a word more. *What is my dream now? What do I want to do with my voice?*

"More coffee?" a waitress came to their table and offered.

"Oh no, time to turn in," Lonny replied for them, and they stood to leave.

They left the diner, which was just across from where they were staying, and walked back to the hotel. Elliot was also coming back, and he held the door open for them.

"It's the crooners coming back for the night," he said, and Ava realized he wasn't alone. He was holding the hand of a tall brunette she recognized from the night's audience.

"Thank you," she said as she passed without trying to stare at the woman.

"You back for the night too?" Lonny asked, going through the door after her and Edwin.

Elliot looked at the woman with him and laughed.

"The night may not be over just yet," he replied, and the woman flashed him an agreeing smile.

"See you all tomorrow," Lonny said, and they all said goodnight and went their separate ways.

Ava looked back as she and Edwin turned the corner. It appeared that Elliott was taking the woman from the audience back to his room.

"I don't think he knew that girl before tonight," she said in a low voice, and Edwin laughed.

They were at their door now, and he unlocked it.

"Probably not. Many people in the world do not live and think as we do," he said. "You should have seen some of the soldiers I knew with those Italian women!"

He laughed again at her horrified face and closed the door behind them.

"Did you?" she gasped.

"Are you kidding? No! I had you to come home to," he said and pulled her to him.

Chapter 43

"Ladies, I hope you remember my daughter, Ava," Victoria called out and silenced the chatting women.

"Mom," Ava said under her breath. "I haven't been away that long."

"Of course, we couldn't forget that face," her aunt Ingrid spoke first. "But it does seem like forever since I've had the privilege of seeing it."

"It's good to have you with us again, dear," Alice Fitzpatrick said next, and Ava smiled.

"Ava, do you remember how to do the roll call?" Victoria asked under raised eyebrows.

"I've only missed a couple of meetings."

"All right, then, we'll let you resume your job, which Myrtle has been gracious to do in your absence."

Myrtle handed Ava the roll call, and she readied her pen to check off each person present, thinking for the hundredth time that her mother could just check the names off herself after the meeting.

"Myrt..," Ava began

"Oh, and when your name is called, please answer present and say what you are looking forward to the most this spring," Victoria interrupted.

"Myrtle Bonds," Ava began again.

"Present and daffodils," Myrtle said as instructed.

"Ingrid Carson."

"More sunshine." Ingrid nodded her baggy cheeks. "And I'm present."

"Abigail Dempsey."

"Present, and I would have to say daylilies."

"Alice Fitzpatrick."

"Present. Greener grass for me."

Ava went down the list until each woman had responded and then put down her pen.

"You didn't tell us what you are most looking forward to this spring," Maris Ingram said.

"Me?" Ava replied. Didn't they know she was there to assist, not participate? "Oh, um, I guess butterflies, yes butterflies." She did love to watch the butterflies fluttering about the butterfly bush next to their front porch. Estelle had planted the bush, which made it even more special.

"What is Elliot King like?" Delores Waters asked next, and Ava was even more surprised by this question. She didn't think most people her parents' age knew much about modern music.

"He's great to work for," she said, looking to her mother to be sure it was appropriate to discuss her band during a garden club meeting. "A true entertainer if I've ever seen one."

"And very handsome," Delores added. Ava laughed, and Victoria cleared her throat.

"Now, how would you know that?" Ingrid asked, and all the other ladies giggled.

"Well, anyone who has seen him in a magazine might have noticed." Delores gave them all a smug smile with her thin lips.

"Let's get to our meeting," Victoria cut in, and the room fell silent again. "Today, we will be discussing fruit trees."

Is he in a lot of magazines? Ava thought as she moved quietly out of her seat and to the table her mother had arranged with dessert plates and fried apples pies. *Will I be mentioned in a magazine with him?* As they discussed apple, peach, and pear trees, Ava piled her plate high with the fried pies her mother seldom made. She guessed they had been chosen to fit this month's topic as the dried apples in them had come from the two apple trees on their property. They were crispy on the outside, moist in the middle, and buttery all over. She didn't care how many she ate today. After what seemed like an interminable time, the talk turned away from fruit trees and to the community.

"I think that Floraline is going to be just as big with this one as she was with the last one," Alice said, and Ava almost choked on her sweet milk.

"Floraline's expecting again?" she blurted out.

"She certainly is. She didn't tell you?"

"I haven't seen her since before Christmas. I mean isn't it really soon for her to have another baby?"

"It happens all the time," Maris said, and the women laughed at what must have been an odd expression on her face. She just couldn't understand how her friend would want another baby so soon. Wasn't she still getting used to the first one?

"Mott is an excited grandmother," Alice went on. "With Margaret's boys getting older, she's anxious for some babies in the family again."

"That she is," Abigail agreed of her sister-in-law.

"Babies do brighten up things." Maris sighed, and a loud sob broke out from beside her. "Myrtle, whatever is the matter?"

"Don't mind me," Myrtle said in between sobs she shook with trying to hold back.

"Enough about babies," Victoria spoke up, and Ava wanted to yell out an "Amen." "With Rosemary's baby due any day now, Myrtle is having a hard time not being with her daughter."

"Oh, I know that is a difficulty." Maris patted her friend on the back.

"I still think it's a shame that husband of hers won't bring her back here for the birth. A girl needs her mother at a time like this," Ingrid put in, and Victoria shot her a threatening look.

"He does have a job to think about," Victoria returned. "Rosemary probably wants her husband nearby for the birth too."

"I suppose so." Ingrid folded her hands in her lap, and Ava hoped that was the end of it.

"I just have to tell you all about a new cake recipe I got from my Aunt Sue," Abigail said as Myrtle blotted her eyes with a tissue and breathed in sharply to get a hold of herself.

"What kind is it?" Alice asked, and everyone but Ava reluctantly joined the less entertaining conversation.

Ava busied herself cleaning up all the dessert plates and cups the women had left sitting about the room. She might not be at the meeting next month, so she had best help her mother all she could. *Who knows when the band will have another weekend off?*

Chapter 44

Rosemary struggled to sit up in bed. Now, she realized that the pain she had been dreaming about was real. She ran her hand over her lower abdomen and then around to her lower back. *Is this it?* When the pain decreased and then completely went away, she figured it was just the "preparatory pains" her mother had warned her about. She thought her actual time was still a couple of weeks away. She looked over at Percy's side of the bed. Of course, he wasn't back yet. It was too early. She would feel better if he was there, but she wouldn't keep him home. It was easier to let him go. If he didn't go, he was restless and unhappy with anything or anyone, including her.

She lumbered over onto her other side and closed her eyes, hoping for undisturbed sleep. It wasn't long before she was dreaming. She and Judith were running together behind their house and then somewhere else she didn't recognize. She stopped, finding it hard to breathe, and watched as her sister ran on without her. Another sharp pain, and Rosemary awoke again. She sat up wondering how long she had been asleep this time. Still no Percy. She rubbed her stomach trying to work out the pain. Again, it went away, and again, she lay back down. On her back now, she stared up at the high ceiling. This time, she couldn't go back to sleep. Minutes passed, and the pain began again. She clenched her fists and cried out now, frightened that what she was feeling had to be actual labor contractions. When those subsided, she lifted her body out of the bed and pulled on her house coat and shoes. She had no choice. She would have to get Mrs. Ramsey.

The door creaked loudly. The house was dark except for the light at the front door. She held on tight to the banister and made her way down the staircase. Halfway down, the pain started again. She sat on the steps and rocked back and forth with it. It lasted longer this time but eventually ebbed away. She stood back up and made her way down the rest of the stairs. She had never been to the Ramseys' bedroom before but knew it was on the other side of the living room. She knocked on the door just as another contraction began. There were shuffling feet now behind the door, and she bit her lip to keep from crying.

"Rosemary!" Mr. Ramsey said in alarm.

"Is it time, sweetheart?" Mrs. Ramsey asked from behind him. She pushed the door all the way open and took Rosemary's bent over body in her arms. "Where's your husband?"

"He's....out," Rosemary answered from behind clenched teeth.

"Oh, heavens!" Mrs. Ramsey said without hiding her consternation. "Let's get you to the hospital. Thomas, leave Mr. Bledsoe a note on the table by the door."

Rosemary held on to Mrs. Ramsey's hand, and she led her back down the hall and out the front door. Thomas jotted down an almost intelligible note for Percy and joined them at the car.

"Go ahead. Squeeze my hand as hard as you like. It does help I've heard," Mrs. Ramsey instructed.

Rosemary tried to smile but failed as another pain caused her body to shudder, and she squeezed the older woman's hand as hard as she could. They helped her into the back seat of their car and took her to Harper Hospital. The rest was a blur of polished halls, white-clad nurses, a tidy bed, and then a young doctor telling her to breathe and push. A nurse had taken Mrs. Ramsey's place, and Rosemary pressed her hand and screamed as she obeyed the doctor's commands. A baby's cry was finally heard, and they gave her some kind of medicine. She didn't even see the child's face before her head hit the pillow.

"You're awake," Percy said when her eyelids opened.

Rosemary stared into his frightened face and then gasped as she remembered where she was. She tried to sit up, but he pushed her back down.

"The doctor says you need to rest." He gripped her hand almost as hard as she had gripped Mrs. Ramsey's hand earlier that night. "You were so still, almost too still. The doctor said you were fine, but..."

"Where's the baby?" she asked, her hazel eyes searching all sides of the room.

"He's with the nurses."

"He?" Rosemary did sit up now whether he wanted her to or not. "It's a boy?"

"Yes, you didn't know?"

"No, they gave me some kind of medicine right after the birth. Is he as beautiful as I imagined?"

"I've only seen him myself through the glass window. They won't let me hold him yet, but yes. How could he not be with you as his mother?" He kissed her hand now. "Rosemary, I'm so sorry I wasn't there last night."

"It's of no matter. I had Mr. and Mrs. Ramsey. Now, will you please get the nurse and ask if I can see our baby?"

"Are you sure you're ready? The doctor said…"

"I'm fine. Well, I will be fine once I see our boy."

"Ok, ok." He stood up.

"Wait?" she called out when his hand was on the door. "Did we agree on a name?"

"The name is all yours, remember?"

"So, you approve of Owen Jude Bledsoe?"

"Yes, he has my last name. There's no reason he shouldn't have some of your family names too."

She smiled now and waved him back to her bedside. He came and bent over her, and she kissed him.

"What's that for?"

"The name," she answered, and he laughed. "Now, go get my baby."

Two days later, Rosemary and the baby were home, and Percy was back at work. Owen lay in the center of their bed on the blue and white knitted blanket Myrtle had made and sent just after Christmas.

"What do you think about this place, Owen?" Rosemary asked her son as his brown eyes looked from her face to the strange room about them.

"I love your eyes," she spoke in the soft voice she used with Judith before she became an unruly toddler. "They are brown like your daddy's but not at all bothered."

He cooed back at her and stretched out his hands and feet. The kerosene heater had made the room warm, so she was letting him lie uninhibited in all but his cloth diaper.

"I love your little toes and fingers too," she told him and cupped his feet in her hands. "They're smaller than Judith's were." She laughed now thinking of her sister as a baby.

"One day you'll meet Judith. I will have to tell her not to be too rough with you."

Owen's eyes were starting to close, so she quit talking. She reached for the stationary, pen, and book on the night stand. She placed a clean sheet of paper on the book to bear down on and gazed back at her son. Her mother would see her baby through her eyes.

When Percy got home from work, he found his wife asleep in her bath robe next to the baby.

"Rosemary," he whispered as he shook her shoulder. He wasn't sure if she wanted Owen awake now or not, but, as soon as he spoke, the baby's face contorted, and he opened his eyes and stared into his father's face.

"Hi there," Percy said to him, and Rosemary sat up, smiling at the interaction.

"For you," he said next and handed his wife a bouquet of mixed flowers.

"Percy, you didn't have to bring me anything," she replied but drew them to her nose despite herself.

"You deserve them. I also brought dinner." He sat a bag of food down on the table. "It's your favorite, meatloaf."

"Thank you. I'm famished."

He now sat down next to her, and she entwined her fingers through his and lay her head on his shoulder. Owen let out a noise that sounded like a hungry gurgle, and they laughed.

"Guess he wants to eat before we do," she said and lifted him into her arms.

"I told the boys that I'm staying home tonight. Let me help you with whatever you need." Percy touched the back of his son's head. His dark hair felt like fine yarn in his hand.

Rosemary smiled at him in response. She had never been happier than in this moment, and even though she knew it wouldn't last, she wished in her heart for him to stay home with them every night.

Chapter 45

Ava stopped with her hand on the door and listened. It was Myrtle's voice reading to her mother.

"Owen is an active infant with eyes full of innocent light. He's always looking around and seeing just what all his hands and feet can do. He's not bald like so many babies but has a crop of black hair that I am afraid may be unruly as he grows. Percy and I are always touching it! He loves to lay close to me but not so close that he can't move about. Oh, how I wish you both could see him for yourself! I am hoping that we can come back and visit once things are more settled. Do you like his name? Dad, Percy insisted that I name him after you and Grandpa Owen. I love you and miss you all very much. Love, Rosemary."

"She and Vivie had the first babies born in a hospital in the family," Victoria said.

"After that dreadful night we lost Estelle, I'm glad of it," Myrtle replied.

"Me too, even though I don't blame us or Dr. Green for that night." There was silence for a moment as they both pushed the memory from their minds. "He does sound like an excellent baby."

"He does. Jude thinks he may look too much like his father, but I only pray he doesn't act like him," Myrtle confided.

"We will be diligent in our prayers," Victoria said, and Ava quietly stepped away from the front door and back down the steps.

She had the baby! Her brain screamed as she ran back to her mailbox. She had been so bent on practicing her music after her classes that she didn't even consider the mailbox when she passed it. She checked it now, and, sure enough, there was a letter from Rosemary inside. She opened it right there and read.

Dear Ava,

I have a boy! He was born on March 9 at 2:42 in the morning. The contractions were painful but not as bad as I thought they would be. Mr. and Mrs. Ramsey got me to the hospital quick.

Ava paused in her reading and narrowed her eyes. *Where was Percy? Why didn't he take you?* She would write and ask. No, what if Percy saw the letter or Rosemary didn't like her questioning her husband.

He is a beautiful boy with dark hair and brown eyes like his father. My only regret is that none of you are here to see him. My heart aches that my family are not some of the first people he meets. Enough moaning. I am happy. Where are you singing next with Elliot King? I wish you had a concert in Michigan! How much longer are you singing with his band? Owen is starting to cry. I think it is time to feed him again. I will write more later on.

Love,
Rosemary

The next afternoon after classes, Ava wandered through Westend Drug Store looking at baby things. Bottles, bibs, teething rings, and pacifiers, she really knew very little about infants. Even when Ella was one and living with them, she only provided a free pair of hands when absolutely needed.

Bibs should work, she thought and selected one in each color. The last time she had seen Floraline, her friend's baby was drooling all over everything, including her mother's Sunday dress. She also couldn't resist the ornate, silver baby spoon lying next to the bibs. It was so shiny that she could see her face in it when she picked it up. Looking at her reflection, she thought again of her own unborn baby.

What kind of mother would I have made? she silently asked the reflection. *There would certainly be no Elliot King Band. That's what happened to Janene Richman.*

Ashamed of her thoughts, she closed the spoon in her hand and went to the counter to pay for Rosemary's gifts. The sales lady wrapped up her purchases, and she hurried out of the store. As soon as she stepped out of the door, her school friend Rebekah was running toward her, waving a magazine in her hand.

"Ava! You're in here! You made the magazine!" Rebekah pushed a copy of Stardom Magazine into her hands and flipped to the next to last page. "Right here! Look! 'Elliot King Tours with New Songstress." She pointed to the upper, right-hand title on the left page.

"It can't be," Ava muttered, disbelieving even the title.

"It's you all right!" Rebekah tapped on her name in the article and then read for her. "Many thought that band leader Elliot King would be unable to replace a singer like Janene

249

Richman, who left the band temporarily to give birth to her son last month, but they were wrong. Mr. King found a previously unknown singer, Ms. Ava Livingston, touring with a smaller band in Alabama. Ms. Livingston's voice has more than filled the vacancy left behind by Ms. Richman. Some even wonder if Ms. Richman will be asked back. The Elliot King Band continues to rise in popularity thanks to Ms. Livingston and to the band leader's popularity with the ladies."

"I just can't believe it." Ava stared at her name on the magazine's page.

"I'm friends with a star!" Rebekah said louder than Ava would have liked, but no one seemed to have noticed them.

"I'm hardly a star."

"Sure you are. You can have this copy to prove it. I'll buy another."

"Thanks." Ava smiled now, her face flushed with the news. "Want an ice cream? I'll buy to pay you back for the magazine."

"I can't refuse a star!" Rebekah laughed.

Ava ate ice cream with her friend and then hurried home with the magazine.

"Well, I'll be darn," Grandpa Chester remarked later that night as he eyed his granddaughter's name in the publication, which was extended as far out as his arm would allow to compensate for his far-sighted vision.

"That's my girl's name!" Sheffield said, reading over his father-in-law's shoulder.

"Let me see it again." Victoria took the copy from her father and began reading aloud, "Mr. King found a previously unknown singer, Ms. Ava Livingston, touring with a smaller band in Alabama."

"Unknown!" Grandpa Chester griped as if the word was an insult.

"I was," Ava said.

"I don't know. I thought that Willie Harold Band was a pretty big deal," Sheffield spoke.

"Just to those in our area," Ava replied.

"Ms. Livingston's voice has more than filled the vacancy left behind by Ms. Richman. Some even wonder if Ms. Richman will be asked back," Victoria read on.

"Now, that part they got right," Grandpa Chester interrupted again.

"You should hear her. She's better than any of them," Edwin said from where he had been standing silently watching them look over the magazine article he had already memorized.

"You've only ever heard me perform." Ava grinned and squeezed her husband's hand.

"The Elliot King Band continues to rise in popularity thanks to Ms. Livingston and to the band leader's popularity with the ladies," Victoria ignored them and read on.

Ava's face reddened at the last part, thinking back to the tall brunette Elliot had taken back to his room and wondering what her mother would think of her boss.

"Delores Waters is certainly one of those ladies," Victoria said, and Ava laughed.

"What does Delores have to do with Elliot King?" Sheffield asked.

"Apparently, she reads about Mr. King frequently in the magazines and thinks he is quite the looker."

Carson laughed, and Ava realized that her disinterested brother had been listening after all.

"Congratulations," he said to her from where he lay on the floor with his hands behind his head and his eyes closed.

"Thanks," Ava replied with hesitation when a joke didn't accompany his remark. She wasn't use to getting compliments from her brother.

"This is certainly high praise." Victoria handed the magazine back to her daughter. "You have done well."

"Thank you," Ava said but knew by her mother's raised eyebrows and taut cheeks that she was thinking more.

"I'm proud of you." Sheffield hugged her.

"So, does this mean you will be continuing on with this band?" Victoria asked.

There it is, Ava thought.

"I don't know," she answered. "We haven't discussed it. I would assume Janene Richman would want her job back, and in a couple of months, the band's performances are moving out of the south."

"She may not want her job back. It's often hard for young mothers to leave their children," Victoria said.

"Couldn't she take the baby with her?"

"On the road, from one place to another? I don't think that would be an ideal arrangement for a baby."

"I think the band members want to keep Ava," Edwin spoke up.

"What are you talking about?" Ava eyed her husband who had never told her this before.

"I talk to them. Lonny and a few others have told me that they want you to stick around."

"And what about your school?" Sheffield asked.

"The summer is almost here, but this is all probably nonsense talk anyway. Janene will more than likely be back, and Elliot won't even ask." Ava threw up her hands to put an end to the conversation. She didn't want to even think of the band interfering with her college classes. Her dad loved to hear her sing, but he loved to see her in college even more.

"It's probably best to at least consider the invitation to stay all the same," Victoria said, and Ava nodded reluctantly.

"Dinnertime yet?" Grandpa Chester asked as a grumble escaped his stomach.

"Finally, someone else is hungry!" Carson got up from the floor as quickly as he had laid down and was the first at the table.

Chapter 46

"Just flip him over on his stomach. My Aunt Shirley always said it's good for babies to practice lifting their heads up a bit. Builds their strength," Mrs. Ramsey said, and Rosemary turned Owen over on his stomach and removed her hand. The little boy's eyes widened as he adjusted to his new position.

"I think he likes it," Annamae said from the other side of the blanket where she and Rosemary sat on the floor with the baby, and the three women laughed as they watched Owen ball up his fists and lift his head first to the right and then to the left.

"He's a strong baby!" Mrs. Ramsey praised.

"Percy will be glad to hear that," Rosemary replied.

Owen continued to lift up and observe everything in sight until his head started to get heavy.

"Can I hold him?" Annamae asked when he began to cry from his effort.

"Sure, I think that's enough exercise for now." Rosemary watched as Annamae scooped up her son from the blanket.

"There, there." Annamae settled him on her lap, and he was already content again staring at her red hair. "Aren't you just the cutest?"

"Thomas thinks so," Mrs. Ramsey said. "He just goes on and on about him. You'd think he had never seen a baby before!"

"That's kind of him." Rosemary smiled, feeling again the new gratitude she felt whenever anyone else took an interest in her son.

"I often wonder what kind of baby Johnny and I will have. Nan said once that between his height and my hair, any baby of ours would probably be a red-headed giant!"

"Oh, you never know. Thomas had a nephew once that came out with hair every bit as red as yours and not a single person in the family had red hair. Come to think of it, that boy always was a little odd." Mrs. Ramsey chuckled as the front door opened and Thomas walked in with the mail.

"Thomas! We were just talking about your nephew Les."

"Les? Haven't seen that strange boy in a while."

"Now, be nice," Mrs. Ramsey chided.

"Rosemary, you have a package." Mr. Ramsey laid down a bundle of letters on the table and handed her a brown paper box.

"It's from my cousin," she said as soon as she saw Ava's cursive handwriting.

"Probably a gift for this little fellow!" Annamae bounced the baby up in her lap, and he cooed at her in response.

They all watched as she opened the box and pulled out a handful of white, blue, yellow, and green bibs.

"Always need bibs with a baby," Mrs. Ramsey said of them.

Rosemary nodded and noticed the shiny silver spoon sitting under them in paper.

"Oh!" she gasped, lifting the little spoon out of the box.

"Look at your new fancy spoon." Annamae turned Owen toward his gift and pointed at it.

"I can't wait to feed you with this," Rosemary told her son, but he appeared to notice something out the window more than what she was holding out to him.

"They just make the loveliest things for babies now," Mrs. Ramsey said. "Is it my turn to hold him yet?"

"Yes, I need to be going anyway." Annamae carefully stood up with the baby and handed him to the older woman. "Johnny will be home before long."

"Actually, I think it's my turn to hold him," Mr. Ramsey said.

"It is certainly not. You held him this morning," Mrs. Ramsey replied, and Rosemary laughed.

"You can both hold him a few minutes before I take him upstairs to feed him," she said.

After Annamae had left and the Ramseys had held Owen, Rosemary sat by herself nursing her baby and reading Ava's letter that had come with the present.

Dear Rosemary,

I can't believe you are a mother! I am glad that the whole birthing thing wasn't as terrible as you thought. Owen sounds delightful! Does he cry a lot like Judith use to do? I still remember the two of us trying to do funny things to calm her. I couldn't imagine your baby being fussy, though. Did your mom tell you that Floraline is expecting again? Two babies so close together! How will she manage with two of them needing her all the time?

I have some news of my own for you. I was written about in Stardom magazine with Elliot King! I never dreamed that something like that would happen to me. If you want to read the article, it is in this month's issue.

I don't know how long I will sing with the band. It was supposed to just be until Janene Richman returned, but no one has mentioned her coming back yet. I'm not sure what will happen. It would be great to sing in Michigan!

Give Owen a kiss for me. Hope he enjoys the gifts. I couldn't resist the pretty spoon!

Love,
Ava

Owen was now finished eating and sleeping in her arms. Rosemary felt his soft breaths on her skin and thought about how different her life and her cousin's life were. She might not be in magazines, but those breaths hitting her neck were the best thing she could ever imagine happening to her. She almost fell asleep herself until she realized the time and that Percy was still not home. She hoped he was late because he was bringing home dinner again. She wasn't up to going out just yet, and she knew he wouldn't want to wait on her to cook. She stood up with Owen, still asleep in her arms, and went to the window. A boy passed on a bike, and a dog barked after him, but Owen kept sleeping. A few cars went by, none with her husband. She stood looking and waiting awhile longer until Owen woke up crying for a diaper change. She listened for the door over his cries as she changed the diaper.

Where is he? Where is he? She kept asking the window he wouldn't appear in. Her stomach began to growl, and she realized again just how late it was. Finally, she tiptoed down the stairs with Owen in her arms. She didn't want to bother the Ramseys or make them aware of her missing husband. Unfortunately, Mr. Ramsey was making a cup of coffee in the kitchen.

"Why there's that sweet, happy boy again!" he greeted, and Rosemary managed a smile that she was afraid wouldn't fool anyone. Thankfully, it was Mr. Ramsey and not Mrs. Ramsey.

Owen stared up at the older man and almost seemed to smile back at him.

"He does like you," she said as she made her way to the pantry shelf with her and Percy's things. She didn't know how much longer she could hold back her worry. She grabbed a half loaf of bread and a banana. She would just eat another banana sandwich for dinner.

"Has Percy not made it back yet?" Mr. Ramsey asked when he saw what she had gotten.

"He's working late," she lied and hated herself for it.

"That's too bad."

"Yes, it is. Have a good night," she said and hurried out before her lie folded under her.

Back in the room, she laid Owen in his bassinet and made her sandwich. She was so hungry she didn't even bother putting it on a plate.

"All of this feeding you is making me hungrier than I've ever been in my life," she told Owen as his eyelids began to droop again.

She made another sandwich and was almost finished eating it when the front door opened and Percy walked in. Her mouth opened to ask where he had been and then closed seeing his appearance. She didn't have to ask. She knew where he had been. He looked and smelled of alcohol, but, surprisingly, his eyes were clear.

"How could you?" she asked in a calm voice despite the suppressed anger her body was shaking with.

"I had to." He walked past her to the bed.

"What do you mean?"

"It's how I handle things. If you really want to know everything, I was suspended for the day for being late for work again. It was either drink or come home and fall apart in front of you."

"How were you late? You left early." She put her hands up to her head not comprehending him.

He looked at her and laughed, and her cheeks blazed.

"I told you. It's how I handle things."

"You've been leaving early in the mornings to drink?" she asked, raising her voice now.

"Why not? That baby has already got me up, and I'm trying to stay home at night for the two of you."

Now, her cheeks drained of all their color. How could he call their son "that baby?"

"Fine, we'll sleep in the other room tonight, and go out whenever you like from now on!"

She lifted up Owen and his bassinet off the floor and, somehow in her anger, managed to open the door too.

"Glad I have my wife's permission," he said after her, and she closed the door to his laughing.

259

Once she was in the other room, which didn't have a kerosene heater, she found two more blankets.

"He does love you," she whispered to Owen, wrapping the blankets around his small body. "That's the alcohol talking, not him."

Once he was settled, she lay out another blanket for herself and collapsed on the floor she had been on once before. This time, however, she was too angry to cry. Having a son had awakened a new protective side of her she didn't even know existed.

Sometime early in the morning, she woke up to find Percy lifting her up off the floor. He was sober now and remorseful. The hateful laugher was gone. She didn't speak as he carried her to their bed and laid her gently down in it. When she noticed that the bassinet with Owen was back by their bed, she let her eyes close again. After a fitful night of tending to Owen and her own anger, her body was demanding sleep. She thought she heard Percy crying into his hands beside her, but she didn't respond. His need for her forgiveness would have to wait. She had to be a mother again when Owen woke up whether she was ready to or not.

Chapter 47

"Two hands on the wheel!" Victoria let out from the passenger side of Ava's Chevrolet Coupe.

"Mom, I was just pushing back my hair with my free hand," Ava replied and didn't bother to silence the sigh that followed.

"In driving, there are no free hands." Victoria continued to concentrate her eyes on her daughter who in turn concentrated her eyes on the road.

"I still can't believe James took off from his classes to have lunch with us," Ava said, trying to turn her mother's attention elsewhere.

"Vivie wrote that his grades are so exceptional that his teachers didn't have any kind of fuss with it at all."

"Mrs. Wheeler arranged everything for me. The semester is almost finished, and she said that since I was practicing my musical skills in a real-life situation, she didn't..."

"Should you be talking this much while you drive?" Victoria interrupted.

"Dad and Carson talk while they drive," Ava replied and sighed even louder.

"Yes, but they are more experienced drivers."

"I have become very experienced over the last three months with Edwin and me driving to concerts!"

261

"And do you two talk every moment you are on the road?"

"Yes, well most of it. Helps to keep you awake too."

"Now, you might have a point. Are you tired? Do we need to pull over?"

"No, I'm just saying that talking helps keep you alert."

"If you keep two hands on the wheel, I guess we can talk." Victoria looked away from her daughter and to the new road they were turning onto. They were taking backroads through Heflin, Alabama and then on into Georgia. Farms were on either side of them, and she smiled at a group of plump cows lying in the sunshine.

"I feel about as lazy as one of those cows just sitting here in the car while your father, grandpa, and brother work."

"Enjoy having a day off for a change," Ava said, glad that maybe their argument over her driving was over.

"Oh, I will. Any day I get to see my grandbabies is a good day!"

"If you want to stay at James's house during the concert, you can," Ava offered.

"And miss hearing you with this new band! Never!" Victoria declared, and Ava smiled at the road ahead. "Besides, I also want to see this man who Delores thinks is so good looking."

"Mom!" Ava laughed.

"What? She'll want to know all about it. Might as well meet the man if I've driven this far to hear his band on a Wednesday."

"Of course, he'll want to meet you. He's very friendly."

"So, I've heard."

"Have you been reading the magazines too?" Ava chanced a look at her mother and caught a guilty arch of the eyebrows.

"Maybe. I have to know what sort of person is employing my daughter."

Ava laughed again and made sure both eyes were back on the road and both hands on the wheel so not to spoil the mood.

Soon, they were driving up to James's house, and Ella with Vivie and the baby in tow were greeting them at the car.

"She hasn't sat still all morning. Couldn't wait for you to get here," Vivie greeted and gave them both one armed hugs around Jacqueline.

"Ella, how I've missed you and your great big hugs!" Victoria picked up the toddler, and Ella gave her a hug around the neck.

"Goodness! Hasn't she grown since Christmas?" Ava said of her other niece who wasn't so bundled up this time and stared at her with unflinching, blue eyes. She had more wisps of blond hair now and looked more like a girl than the last time Ava had seen her.

"I'm your aunt Ava." Ava took one of the baby's hands in hers and smiled.

"Yes, she has grown. She must still be eating well," Victoria said, putting Ella down. She started to reach for the baby, but Ella pulled on her arm.

"Come in! See my tea cups!" she squealed.

"Certainly," Victoria replied, and they all laughed.

"Hello, Mom, Ava," James called out, and they noticed him at the door now. With his hands in his pants'

263

pockets and his white undershirt, he looked more relaxed than Ava had seen him in years.

"There's that banjo-playing son of mine!" Victoria put her arms around her son despite Ella. "I was happy to hear that your professors let you miss class. Vivie said your grades are exceptional."

Ava frowned behind her. She knew that was all she would hear from both her parents for the next few weeks.

"He studies enough for them to be," Vivie interjected, and Ava noticed a tinge of displeasure in her usually over cheerful voice.

"That's what school is for," Victoria said as they were led into the house.

"I've started lunch but need to fry the pork chops. Would you mind taking the baby?" Vivie asked, and Victoria gladly took Jacqueline as Ella brought in a sack of colorful tea cups.

"Thank you," Ava said, taking a little green and pink-flowered tea cup from her niece. "This looks delicious. What is it?" She stuck out her pinky and pretended to take a sip from the cup.

"Lemonade," Ella replied.

"I think we're raising a waitress," James said, and Ella looked up at her father in surprise. She had given everyone but him a cup. "Don't I get a cup?" he asked.

Ella smiled and set a yellow and blue-flowered cup in his hand, and he also pretended to take a drink.

"Best thing to drink I've had all day!" James praised, and his daughter laughed now.

"I'll take a refill," Ava said.

"Not before I get another one!" James cut in, and Ella laughed almost as loud as her stepmother could.

Ava noticed Vivie had come back, wiping her hands on a dish towel, to see what was so funny. All three women laughed as they watched James gulp down the pretend drink again. It was the playful James they all loved so much and rarely saw.

"I guess I better get a cup of that," Victoria said and accepted a blue and white-flowered teacup from her granddaughter.

"I'll have to drink mine later." Vivie winked at Ella and went back to the kitchen.

"How's the farm going?" James asked.

"Planting more soybean," Victoria answered. "It seems Pete had a good idea."

"Old Pete! Didn't know he had any wisdom in him!" James laughed at the idea of his brother's school friend giving his parents helpful advice.

"Well, he does it appears. Soybeans are much cheaper to plant than cotton. Your father is barely planting any cotton at all this year."

"He and Floraline are having another baby," Ava said.

"Good for him."

"I don't see how two that close together can be any good!"

"You and Carson were pretty close together," Victoria spoke up.

"And that had to be difficult!" James laughed. "Jimmy came through Atlanta not long ago," he spoke of his brother's other boyhood friend now.

"Still sorry for his poor mother that he stayed in the military," Victoria said.

"Why? He travels the world, eats well. He's happy."

"If you say so."

"He does think we're headed for another war, though."

"Now, don't you go sounding like your father! Let's not even talk about wars with these sweet babies here."

"Ok, I won't say anything to sully the little ones, but Jimmy and Dad might be right."

"Not if my prayers have anything to do with it!" Victoria gave her son a stern look and then smiled down at the baby in her arms. "Jacqueline, you are the spitting image of your mother."

"Neither one of my girls look like me. They both took after their mothers," James said, and Ella looked up again, realizing that her father was talking about her.

"Thank the good Lord for that," Victoria agreed. "You couldn't ask for them to be any prettier!"

"So, you're performing at the Fox Theatre this time?" James turned to his sister.

"Yep."

"Fancy place," he said and whistled.

"I can't imagine it being any fancier than the Georgian Terrace."

"That's because you haven't seen the Fox yet. Took Vivie to a movie there on one of our first dates."

"Yes, he did. It was *Duel in the Sun*, and he had to drag me out." Vivie was back in the room, a smile brightening her face with the memory.

266

"We were the last ones out the door. Had to practically carry her out," James remembered, and Vivie's laugh filled the room.

Ava saw her mother cringe with its noise. There were somethings about her daughter-in-law she would never get used to.

"You'll love the Fox. It's so romantic!" Vivie said. "Ready for lunch?"

After a plate full of fried pork chops, cabbage, and lima beans, Ava and Victoria said their reluctant goodbyes, and Ava was on her way to sing at the "romantic" Fox Theatre. She hoped her food would settle before Elliot expected her to start warming up. She didn't like to eat a lot before a performance, and her body felt heavy as she followed the driving directions her mom was reading her, which were a mixed up jumble of what Elliot had written to her and James had filled in. The theater was located on Peachtree Street right across from the Georgian Terrace and easy to find, however. She had been enamored by its outside facade last year, but pulling up to it now, she felt as though she were really seeing it for the first time.

"What's the matter?" Ava asked when her mother gasped.

"Maybe, Vivie was right about this place," Victoria said. "Look at the road, Ava, not the building!"

"I am," she lied.

With the building's grand entrance and mosque-like architecture it looked like it belonged in another time and place. Even in the day time, Ava could imagine the building all lit up and welcoming couples and families inside for a night of entertainment.

They found a place to park along the street, and Ava and Victoria walked through the theater's arcade. Gold was all Ava could see as her eyes swept the walls and fixtures. The color was everywhere, adorning and giving a richness to each detail.

At the door, a theater worker began to direct them to the ballroom where Elliot King's band was rehearsing when Lonny came by.

"Ava!" he greeted and hugged her.

"Mom, this Lonny Sands, the other singer in our band," Ava introduced.

"The way my daughter and son-in-law talk about you, I feel like I already know you," Victoria said as he gave her a hug as well.

"Same here," he agreed. "We're in the Egyptian Ballroom."

He led them down the long hallway to the room.

"Have you started rehearsing?" Ava asked.

"The guys have started warming up, but Elliot hasn't asked me to do anything yet. I was actually out looking for a snack when you got here."

"You should have eaten lunch with us at my sister-in-law's. We're stuffed, almost too stuffed to sing."

They were at the door to the ballroom now and walked in. Victoria gasped even louder this time, and Lonny laughed.

"Different, right?" he leaned in and said over the band.

"More like amazing," Ava replied.

"I don't know. I find the Pharaoh on the stage a little odd."

There was indeed a golden Pharaoh engraved in the wall behind the stage.

"They say he's Ramses II, the most powerful Egyptian Pharaoh to ever live," he explained.

"Then we should sound even better tonight!"

"I guess." Lonny laughed. "I'm going back out to find something to eat. I'll see you soon."

He ducked back out the door, and Ava and Victoria walked toward the stage with the Pharaoh. The band was playing while Elliot tapped his music stand. Again, Ava was drawn to the color gold, but there were also deep purples and regal reds, which made the room appear both ancient and modern all at once. Circular tables with red-cushioned chairs made a semi-circle around the dance floor in front of the stage with one long table protruding from the center. Candles were already set on the tables ready to give the room an even more profound glow. As they neared the stage, Ava stared up at the Pharaoh. He was scantily clad and waving an imperious hand over a servant of some sort.

"There are so many instruments," Victoria said in her ear, and Ava noticed that her mother cared little for the Pharaoh. Her eyes were taking in the many instruments and their players which made neat rows across the stage.

The band's practice song came to a crashing conclusion, and Elliot raised his arms.

"Just like that tonight," he instructed.

A few of the band members waved down at them, and Elliot realized their presence.

"Ava! Mrs. Stilwell!" he called down and then jumped off the stage to join them.

Recognizing that they had just been given a break, the stage of instrumentalists erupted with chatter where music had been a few moments ago.

"Lonny said you haven't needed us yet. I hope I'm not late," Ava said.

"No, we'll warm you up next. Mrs. Stilwell, it is an honor to have you with us tonight. I hear Ava got her musical talent from you." Elliot took her hand in his and held it for a moment, and Ava could have sworn her mother blushed.

"Both myself and my husband love to sing, so I'm afraid she didn't have a choice in the matter," Victoria replied.

"I may have to get you up on the stage before the night is over!"

Victoria did blush now, and Ava suppressed a laugh. Her mother would already have much to tell Delores Waters.

"Mrs. Stilwell, the room is yours while we practice. Sit anywhere you like."

"Thank you," Victoria replied.

"Ready, Ava?" Elliot asked, jumping back up on the stage.

"I suppose," she said, glad that her stomach didn't feel quite as heavy any more.

Ava warmed up, and then Lonny returned, and they both warmed up. Victoria sat transfixed below them drumming her foot with every beat until it was time for them to all change clothes and be in position for the night's event.

"Who's exactly coming to this concert?" Victoria asked, helping her daughter pull over her head the pale pink gown she had worn once before in Atlanta.

"Business men, I think. Someone mentioned that The Coca-Cola Company is putting the event on."

Ava began brushing her hair, and Victoria unwrapped the dress she had brought to change into. It was her nicest Sunday dress.

"Mom, I wish you would have let me buy you a new dress for tonight," Ava said.

"It's foolish to spend money like that on one night."

"Who said it had to be for one night? You could have worn it the next time we go to Birmingham or at Christmas."

"Just worry about yourself," Victoria said as she put on the familiar blue dress. It may have been simple, but it looked far fancier than it was on her mother whose face always held enough pride to belong in any room.

Soon, the event began, and they were all back in the ballroom with hundreds of other well-dressed strangers. Elliot had somehow arranged for Victoria to sit at the left-hand table closest to the stage. She sat there now watching as her daughter and Lonny took center stage.

"Come on and confess," sang Lonny.

"Why don't you try and guess," Ava sang back.

"Do tell. Let's tell," they sang together.

"Confidentially," Lonny began again.

"Between you and me," Ava returned.

"Confidentially, I love somebody," their voices slipped together in perfect unison. The song was routine now, yet sounded fresh each time they performed it together.

"I've got news for you." It was Lonny's turn.

"Love somebody," Ava sang.

"I feel that way too."

"Love somebody."

"I'm glad it's true.

"That somebody that I love is you!" they finished together, and the room erupted in applause with Victoria clapping the loudest of all. She knew her daughter could sing but not to the extent that she had just heard. Her voice had obviously grown bigger and stronger since their days of singing together as a family at church revivals.

The event went by quicker than weekend ones. Too many of the attendees had early morning responsibilities the next day. There had been less dancing and more dining and watching. Ava said her goodbyes quickly as she and her mom had an almost two-hour drive back home. Elliot caught her by the arm below the stage just as she was about to leave.

"Thanks for coming out today," he said.

"Sure, Atlanta was close enough," she replied. It had been her first mid-week performance with the band, and she had enjoyed getting to see James and Vivie and have her mother with her.

"I spoke to Janene last night. She wants more time with her baby. Could you stay on through the summer? We have a busy schedule, and the band needs you, Ava." His brown eyes pleaded in a way that almost made her uncomfortable.

"When you say a busy schedule, do you mean concerts throughout the week?"

"We've got bookings all over the place, all days of the week. You would be away from home more, but without school during the summer, that wouldn't matter."

Even though Ava had been half expecting his request, she still didn't know what to say. Of course classes would be over for a while, but she had a husband and a home that did matter.

"I'll let you know this weekend in Columbia," she said, careful not to give a look that promised one way or another.

"Ok, but do say yes." He squeezed her arm. "You've got real talent, the best female voice I've ever worked with in fact. You wouldn't regret it."

It was Ava's turn to blush now. Did he really mean his words or was he just trying to persuade her?

"I'll talk to Edwin about it."

"Of course." He smiled now.

"See you this weekend," she said and rushed off to find her mother before he could say anymore.

What will Edwin say? Her mind raced with the unanswered question and her own ambivalent emotions. There would be no way for him to still be with her at nearly every performance. *Is that what I want?*

Chapter 48

It was 5:00 in the morning, and Ava still couldn't sleep. She lay there listening to crickets and Edwin breathe as her mind contemplated Elliot's invitation to keep singing with the band. On the way home from the concert, she hadn't been able contain it. She would have preferred to have talked to her husband or father about it first, but her mother was there, sitting beside her during the dark car ride home. Surprisingly, she had been just as indecisive and did not give her a hearty speech as to why she should stay home with her husband and not go on the road with the band. She supposed her mother's mind was still overcome by the band's "many instruments." Her mother's main complaint was that she would often be the lone female on a bus with "all those men." She had reminded her mother that "all those men" knew her husband and that Edwin was even friends with a good many of them.

"I suppose they are good, well-behaved fellas," Victoria had said, her face invisible in the dark, and Ava didn't bother to tell her that some were and others were just the ones she had worked so hard to keep her away from all her life.

"You still awake?" Edwin asked, and Ava jumped. She hadn't noticed the change in his breathing.

"Are you sure you want me to go with the band?"

He pulled her to him, and she laid her head on his bare chest.

"I never want you to go," he answered, "but I do want the whole world to hear my Songbird sing."

"Right there, you said you want me to stay and go. Which is it?"

"Go! You have to, Ava."

"Why?"

"Because God made you to sing, and I won't stop you."

"But I was also made to be your wife."

He laughed now.

"Do you plan to stop being my wife as soon as you leave?"

"No, of course not." She didn't laugh back. "But wives just don't leave their husbands for weeks at a time."

"Don't worry. I'll be there every weekend I can possibly make it."

"You silly man! We'll spend a fortune on gas."

"Then I guess you need to ask Elliot for a raise."

She did laugh now.

"He'll give me one."

"I know he will." He caressed her back with his fingers. "You waited for me to come home from the war. Now, it's my turn to wait on you. I'll be here just like you were here for me."

She didn't respond. Instead, she slid up in his arms and kissed him. She would have to sleep later, after class and after her mind was at rest.

Three weeks later, classes were finished for the summer, and Ava stood looking about her house as if it was the last time she would ever see it. Even with the two large

275

suitcases by the door, it was hard to believe that she wouldn't be back tonight.

Is this how James felt when he left for the Army? She remembered how lonely Estelle was in the house without James and how hard she had tried to keep her sister-in-law company. Her hand went to her heart as a pang of sadness came over her at the thought of Edwin coming home after work without her being there. *How can I do this to him, by choice?* For a moment, she was ready to unpack and quit the band altogether. She even stepped toward the ready suitcases, but the front door stopped her.

"All packed?" Sheffield popped his head in and asked.

"I suppose."

"She better be all packed," Victoria said, coming into the house after her husband. "The bus leaves at ten o'clock."

"It's just hard to leave him."

"It won't be for long, just the summer months, and then you'll be back here for him and school," Sheffield replied as he too looked about the clean house she was leaving behind.

Ava swallowed hard. Her father would be the one thinking about her education.

"And don't you worry about Edwin," Victoria said. "We'll keep him well fed when he's here and not traipsing about the country after you. He won't be eating tomato sandwiches by himself every night."

"I know," Ava replied.

"Welp, let's get your bags. Carson is bringing the car around to take you," Sheffield said.

He carried her bags out the door, Victoria followed, and Ava closed the door behind them. The day was bright and harsh with no wind in the air. She squinted at the car as her brother it drove around. Carson parked, and her grandfather emerged from the passenger side.

"My Annie!" he called out. "How are we going to get along around here without you?"

"Don't go changing her mind. She's having a hard enough time as it is," Victoria said.

"I'll miss you this summer." Ava hugged her grandfather as Carson opened the trunk and her father put in the overstuffed suitcases.

"Come back, you hear." Grandpa Chester made her promise.

She nodded as her eyes blurred with tears.

"She's coming back. She couldn't stay away from us all that long," Sheffield said and hugged her next. He held her longer than her grandfather had. He had expected to say goodbye to his sons but not his daughter.

"We need to leave now if we're going to make it," Carson spoke up from where he impatiently stood with one leg already back in the car.

Sheffield let her go, and her mother gave her a quick hug.

"Take care of yourself. Eat all your meals and keep to yourself on that bus," Victoria instructed, and Ava sighed.

"I'll see you all as soon as I can. Elliot said we may get a mid-summer break." She tried to sound as cheerful as she didn't feel at the moment. Saying goodbye to Edwin earlier that morning had been even harder, and she hoped he hadn't been late for work. At least, she would see him in St. Louis the weekend after next.

Sheffield opened the passenger side door for her, and she climbed into the car next to Carson. He immediately cranked it, and before anyone could say anything more, she was waving at her mother, father, and grandfather as the car drove away.

"Where you headed to first?" Carson asked now that they were alone.

"Philadelphia."

"And next?"

"Baltimore," she answered, wondering if her brother wanted a full itinerary. A few days ago, the thought of seeing so many new places had been exciting, but today, it just made her realize how far away she would be from everyone she loved.

"Going to Germany soon?" Ava asked before he could quiz her anymore about her plans.

"What?" he returned.

"You write to there enough. Thought you might have plans to visit."

"I wish," he said, and Ava looked over at him. That wasn't the truthful response she had expected.

"You love that woman don't you?"

He glanced over at her now, his face answering before his mouth.

"Go ahead and say it. I know you do," she prodded.

"Her name is Maria."

"And?"

"And what?"

"You love her."

Carson just studied the road ahead, his face reddening.

"Think you might get to go to Detroit?" he asked instead.

"Elliot hasn't mentioned Detroit. So, I don't think so. Would be nice to see Rosemary."

"Do you think she's happy?" He often thought of the night he had been tasked with talking to Percy and his failure at persuading him to leave Rosemary alone.

"Yes and no, but she does love Percy, and sometimes, that's all that matters," Ava replied. "It's not your fault, Carson. You did just as she asked. Some things just aren't meant to be, I guess." They were both thinking of Jake now.

"Think we'll ever see her again?"

"What a terrible thing to even say! We'll see her again one day. She hopes to bring the baby for a visit." Even as Ava said the words, however, she realized that she didn't have any high hopes of seeing her cousin anytime soon. Then, a worse thought came to her. What if Rosemary did come back while she was away?

"While I'm gone, think you could play checkers with Edwin or take him fishing or something?" she asked.

Carson just laughed at first.

"I suppose I could play him at checkers since you won't be around to beat."

"Hey now! I think you're forgetting our last game!" She laughed too.

"Or you're just remembering it wrong."

They were in Anniston now approaching the bus stop, and Ava could already see the silver and blue bus ready to take her to Philadelphia to meet the band. Carson parked the car along the road, and she sat there a moment longer as he got her bags out of the trunk. *What am I doing?*

"It's only a paper moon, sailing over a cardboard sea," Ava sang under her breath. She didn't know why the song popped in her head. It wasn't even her song. It was Lonny's song or rather Nat King Cole's song. "But it wouldn't be make believe, if you believe in me." That's why she was going, because her husband and her parents believed in her. They wanted her to follow the music and see how far it would take her.

"Are you coming or not?" Carson opened the car door and said.

"You sure are ready to get rid of me!" she muttered back and stepped out into the sunny day again.

"The sooner the better." He grinned down at her as he picked the suitcases back up.

They walked to the bus together.

"Philadelphia, miss?" A hefty man in a snug uniform greeted her.

"Yes," she answered, and he took her bags.

"Have a good trip," Carson said and gave her a hug that was almost too quick to have happened. They laughed. They weren't the hugging sort.

"Thanks for bringing me. See you before too long."

"Ready, miss?" The bus driver asked, returning from storing her bags.

She nodded and boarded the bus. It was warm, and she was glad she had worn a light dress. She walked past a couple with a sleeping baby, a man reading a newspaper, and a woman knitting with a young, already bored girl beside her. She slipped into the seat just behind the last with her purse and a brown paper sack full of books, stationary, hard candy, and anything else she had thought of to keep herself entertained during the long hours. She must have been the last to board, because the bus was already moving. She looked up and out the window. Carson was still standing there. His crew-cut hair had grown out a bit, and with his sunburned cheeks and rolled-up sleeves, he was her brother, the outdoor-loving farmer, right now, and not the clean preacher ready to right the world. He waved, and she waved back.

"It's a Barnum and Bailey world, just as phony as it can be. But it wouldn't be make believe, if you believe in me," she hummed to herself as Carson's face blurred and then disappeared. They all believed in her, and now, she would believe in herself.